PIMCHAN AND AMIRA

TWO STORIES OF POVERTY, WAR, HEARTBREAK AND HOPE

MARGARET NYHON

WILLOW PRESS

Published by Willow Press

Contact author: margaretf@hotmail.co.nz

A catalogue record for this book is available from the National Library of New Zealand.

CONTENTS

AUTHOR'S NOTE

I wrote these two stories to open our minds to what is happening in different parts of our world — how people in distant countries have to fight just to survive from one day to the next, not knowing if they will even have a tomorrow. All they have left is hope. We are so far removed from all these atrocities, something for which we must be truly grateful. But let us not forget those who suffer on a daily basis. Poverty and war were the two horrors that faced two young girls, but resilience and hope in what they believed set them on their separate paths.

Pimchan is based on a true story of the life of a young Thai girl born into poverty, and her sad life in Thailand before meeting a Western lad and going to New Zealand to begin a new life. I personally know Pimchan and James and felt that by telling their story it would open readers' minds to why so many Asian girls want to leave a life of poverty in the hope of a better life elsewhere. But there is a cultural difference. They are tied to families who come first and foremost, which is foreign thinking to our Western culture. Life was not plain sailing for this couple and it comes through in my story.

Amira is a fictional story but the situation on which it is based is only too real. Much has been spoken about the Kurds, but do we know anything about them? Are they friends or foe? Through this story, tirelessly researched, I want people to understand the challenges they have been confronted with.

Who are the Kurds, where do they live and why are they alienated by Middle Eastern countries? There doesn't seem to be a specific reason other than their religious beliefs and perhaps that they were once mountain dwellers who farmed livestock. They have no homeland so at the moment they are refugees in several Middle Eastern countries. They became America's ally in the fight to eradicate ISIS and were promised a Kurdish state. But in 2019, after a meeting with the Turkish leader, US President Donald Trump suddenly announced he was withdrawing his troops from Syria, which left the door open for Turkish soldiers to enter and slaughter Kurdish civilians. It was a despicable act by America, betraying the Kurds with the promise of their own homeland.

While Amira is a fictional character, the YPJ movement and all it stood for is true, as is the fact that the Kurdish people were stripped of their culture. No one wants these people. Will they be 'forever refugees'?

Margaret Nyhon
March 2020

I

PIMCHAN'S JOURNEY FROM POVERTY

Pimchan, your name translates to
'A beautiful moon',
But behind your amazing smile,
A mysterious silence looms.

INTRODUCTION

This story begins in Thailand in the year of 1980. Pimchan was born in the little village of Kantharalak situated on the Thai side of the Mekong River, the boundary separating Thailand from Laos. This was never a peaceful settlement for long, as the echoing of gunfire often rang out across the land, or cannons would open fire over the ownership of the land surrounding the Preah Vihear temple in Cambodia. This was in dispute between the Thai and Cambodian border patrols and had been so for many years. Thailand is surrounded by Laos, Cambodia and Myanmar.

The Preah Vihear (meaning sacred shrine) held the most impressive location of any temple in Cambodia — in isolation, standing sentinel at the top of a cliff, with nothing surrounding it for miles. The Thai government regarded the temple, which faces north, as being built to serve the Sisaket region, a province of Thailand. It was unusual for a Cambodian temple to sit on the north–south axis, rather than aligning with east and west. Early maps had shown it as part of Thailand. However, a boundary survey conducted by the French for the Franco-Siamese Treaty of 1907 deviated from the agreed-upon international divide by watershed — water divide — in order to place the temple on the French Cambodian side. In 1962 the Thai government agreed to submit the dispute to the International Court of Justice, which awarded the temple to Cambodia. Access to the temple is principally from Thailand, as the ruins are difficult to reach from the Cambodian plains at the bottom of a sheer cliff several hundred metres below. An area of 4.6 square kilometres adjourning the temple is claimed by both countries, and even today sees sporadic clashes between Thai and Cambodian border patrols.

The small settlements situated close to the Laos and Cambodian borders were usually very poor, as many of the village people were originally from across the borders. Many thousands of Laos people were displaced during the Khmer Rouge wars, and the Second World War, and when they ended, Laos would not allow their people to return to their own country, so the Thai government let them stay and settle in Thailand. Thousands of people were forcibly relocated and were considered as 'war slaves' who were to serve as 'serfs'. Serfdom is the status of many peasants under feudalism, a collection of debt bondage for the Thai elite. Many thought of a better life over the border, but this wasn't always the case, as there were many poor Thai people in a similar position. The rural poor who lived in these villages on the outskirts were the forgotten people, and their lives were quite primitive.

At the end of the Vietnam War in the early 1970s, as many as one third of the Hmong population left Laos and fled across the Mekong River into Thailand, fearing for their safety if they stayed in Laos. The Hmong traditionally occupied the strategic highlands in Laos, overlooking North Vietnam, and had been traditional enemies of lowland Vietnamese. They entered the conflict against the Vietnamese, first as scouts for the French and later as guerrillas for the Americans. Many Hmong wanted to become Thai citizens, but the Thai government would not allow this to happen.

In 2009, Thailand worked on evicting and resettling hundreds and thousands of Hmong, who had crossed the Mekong River from Laos into Thailand, back across the border, as they were lingering reminders of the Vietnam War.

1

PIMCHAN'S LIFE AS A CHILD

PIMCHAN'S FAMILY was one of those poor Thai families. She lived with her parents and older brother Chetak and her older sister Lawana. Her father was in the army and he married a Laos girl — Pimchan's mother — and brought her across the border. They settled in Kantharalak where some of her father's siblings lived; they were also quite poor. There was very little work in the area, perhaps some seasonal jobs, but very few permanent placements, so most of these village people shared what they had. They had to, otherwise how were they to survive? Pimchan's father had been in the army for many years so owned his own piece of land and a small house. In his mid-life he developed a liking for alcohol, which in the end led to his dismissal from the army. This left no money to support his family, as no benefits of any kind were available to these people. The only help available for Pimchan's father was to go to the temple and live with the monks who would work on curing him. This left the mother to care for her three children. No money, no food, thus forcing her to became the family food-gatherer.

Each morning she would leave the house with her basket and long pole. Depending on what food was available, dictated when she would return home, but she never came back empty-handed. Anything was better than nothing. These people were resilient. They lived a basic life, in fact it was a life of survival, so whatever the mother returned with, the children ate. There were plenty of bugs — cockroaches, grasshoppers, beetles, ants — as well as frogs, rats and silkworms, whatever she could find on the land. She would even climb into bushes searching for food. Her long pole was used for several things, including prodding into bees' nests to get honey, and as a fishing rod to catch fish from the irrigation ponds, which were used to flood the rice paddy fields. The children had to entertain themselves during the day if they didn't attend school, but as most of the village people lived this way, all the children played together; it was a form of communal living. On Pimchan's parents' little block of land there were hens and a buffalo and enough room for a clothesline.

Not everyone was this poor, as the odd foreigner — German or Italian — who had married into Thai families was appearing in the village. They were the new type of landowners, the owners of the rice fields and newly developing tree plantations. Sometimes Pimchan's mother was paid to walk their buffalo along the roadside to feed on the long grass that had not been grazed. She carried a thick stick to prod the animals, and also for protection. This was another way for her to make a little money, as she was on to anything that she was paid for. It was not unusual for the village people to follow the buffalo and search their droppings for the dung beetles. During the rice paddy planting season, there was work in the rice fields for those village people who wanted to work.

Their little house was built with 8 x 1 flitched timber. Four concrete poles were rammed into the ground and this was the main structure to keep the house off the ground for when the monsoon rains arrived. The thatched roof was made of woven coconut palm leaves. Not a lot of words were spoken in Pimchan's home, by either her mother or her father. They lived in relative silence simply because there was little to discuss, as their life was one of mere existence. If anything was spoken it was usually angry words from her mother to her father because of his drinking, but she was away most of the day gathering food. He was the child-minder. School was there for those who could afford to pay, but the village children were more often not at school. Pimchan was eager to learn, but if she arrived at school without money for her teacher, she was sent home, which made her sad, as she was a good student. The English language was just beginning to be taught at the school. Boys' education was far more important than girls'.

Today, Pimchan was not at school as she had no money to give to the teacher. She left the house with her mother to gather food. She carried the basket and her mother carried the long pole as it was too awkward for her to manage.

They walked until they came across a patch of mango trees; this was red ant territory. Her mother lifted the pole when she saw an ant nest and pushed it between the branches hoping to dislodge it. When the nest did manage to fall to the ground, Pimchan picked it up and put it in the basket. Hopefully there were ant eggs inside the nest, as these were served as part of a salad as they had the general appearance of rice. Next, they found bamboo worms. These were the most popular edible insects among the locals, and they were Pimchan's favourite. It was that time of the year for the locust to start arriving and she found some on the long grasses, so tried to grab them, but they were playing games with her, not wanting to be caught. The ones that didn't escape were put inside a bag. Because these were a pest to the agriculture industry, it was a successful method of pest control. When fried, this sort of food became crunchy and tasty. Insects were a rich source of protein, calories, vitamins and minerals.

Sociocultural and economic limitations often prevented the use of pork and beef, thus forcing the poor to eat edible insects, which were readily available and commonly eaten by the rural sector. Urban and educated people were less likely to eat insects, as this was a food source mainly for the poor, creating a learned bias against eating them. More than fifty species of insects are edible in Thailand. When the locust was in full flight, food was plentiful. Tonight, Pimchan's mother would deep-fry the locust and make a papaya salad with green papaya, tomato, lime juice, chilli and the ant eggs with a little added fish sauce. This was a popular dish. Vegetables and herbs grew well in the area.

Each morning between 7 am and 8 am, the traditional walk of the monks — the alms walk — began with the ringing of bells to let the village people know they were coming. They walked the streets with their offering bowls and all the village people would put some food in. This ritual happened every morning. No matter how poor the people were, they all gave food to the monks, even if it was a small amount of rice, as this earned them a higher place in the next life; they became closer to God. This is what everyone strived for. The monks would walk in rows, barefooted in their orange robes, all the time chanting and ringing their bells. They would take the food back to the temple, chant to the Buddha, then everyone at the temple would be fed. Later in the morning, the poorer village people could come to the temple after the monks had eaten and if there was any food left, they would take it home.

2

THE LIFE OF A MONK

AFTER THE DECLINE of Buddhism in India, missions of Sinhalese monks gradually converted over the next two centuries to bring 'Theravada' Buddhism to the Bamar people in Thailand, Laos and Cambodia, where it supplanted previous forms of Buddhism. The Buddhist architecture of Thailand is similar to that in other South-East Asian countries, particularly Cambodia and Laos, with whom Thailand shares a cultural and historic heritage. Thai Buddhism is distinguished for its emphasis on short- or long-term ordination for every Thai man and its close inter-connection with the Thai state and culture.

Monks begin their career as temple boys and start with minor housework duties. The primary reason for becoming a temple boy is to gain basic education in reading and writing as well as memorisation of the scriptures. Prior to state-run primary schools in Thailand, village temples served as the primary form of education for most Thai boys. Service in the temple as a temple boy was a necessary prerequisite for attaining any higher education and was the only learning available to most Thai peasants. After a period of one to three years, most young monks return to secular life, going on to marry. Young men in Thailand who have undergone ordination are seen as being more suitable partners for marriage. A period as a monk is a prerequisite for many positions in leadership: village elders, doctors, spiritual priests, astrologists and fortune tellers. Most men can be ordained as monks for even short periods of time.

Today was the day Pimchan's brother, Chetak, started his time in the temple as a novice. He was taken to his dormitory where he donned his white clothes. They will be trained in ethics and Buddhism, which is good for them and keeps them out of trouble. The first important ceremony for Chetak was to have his hair shaven off including his eyebrows. This was followed by a parade through town to visit the city pillar. At the shrine he made an announcement to the spirits of the shrine that he was ordaining for His Majesty the King. The difference between a novice and a monk is that a novice only has ten precepts to follow, while a monk has two hundred and twenty-seven. After finishing this, the novices changed into their orange robes, under which they wear no underwear, just their robe, and one shoulder is left uncovered. At the end of the ceremony, the abbot read the ten precepts of which Chetak had to repeat. He had to abstain from eating substantial food from noon to dawn, dancing, singing, music, the use of garlands, perfumes or personal adornment like jewellery, soft beds or seats, or accepting any money offered to him. Their day began at 4 am, with meditation for an hour followed by an hour of chanting, then they left their temple to begin their alms walk, a daily ritual to receive food from the people. Thus began Chetak's life as a novice monk.

Pimchan's father had finished his stint at the temple with the monks and was sober once again. This had happened many times before, but he never seemed to be completely cured, as he always slipped back into his old habit. Because they couldn't afford to buy bottles of alcohol there was a simple answer: walk down to the store and buy a nip of whatever and drink it over the counter! This way there was no evidence that one had been drinking. It was the same if one wanted a cigarette: buy one at a time. This was how things were sold, it was the only way these people could have these luxuries.

On the days Pimchan could afford to attend school, she was happy as she was a good student, thus earning her the rights to a scholarship, but before she could accept this, her parents had to pay money upfront. As they didn't have any access to money, the scholarship had to be passed over, thus bringing big disappointment for Pimchan, as she was keen to learn. Now it meant she would have to leave school and find a job to support her parents.

3

PIMCHAN LEAVES HOME

AT AGED FIFTEEN, Pimchan had to leave home and find work in Bangkok. Her father was back at the temple with the monks, as he had borrowed money from family members and it had to be paid back. It was now up to her to find a job and send money home, so his debt could be repaid. Chetak was still at the temple as a monk, but his time was nearly up and he then would have to find work. Because Pimchan had no higher education as such, she would have to look for a job in the textile industry, in the form of a sweatshop. A sweatshop is a factory or workshop, especially in the clothing industry, where manual workers are employed at very low wages for long hours under poor conditions and where they are treated unfairly. But Pimchan didn't have a choice, she had to take work where she could get it.

Two days later, after having slept rough in Bangkok and mingling with hundreds of young girls, with no one bothering to speak, she managed to get a job as a machinist in a sweatshop factory. All she had was her backpack with very few clothes, a blanket and a little single gas cooker, as she had heard about the conditions in the factories. She couldn't afford board, so she would have to sleep on the factory floor along with other young girls who were in the same predicament. This was meant to be a short-term solution until she found somewhere to live, but this did not happen, as was the same for other girls. They simply didn't make enough to afford board. She had enough money to buy a bag of rice, peppers and fish sauce at the markets, before making her way to her place of employment. This would have to do until she received her first pay. The building was four storeys with very few windows; the ones she could see were very high. She doubted those working inside would be able to see out.

She had to walk down a narrow alleyway between two buildings. It was untidy and smelly and there were young men hanging out everywhere. 'They must work in the building on the other side of the alley,' she thought. Girls were lining up waiting for the factory doors to be opened. 'These must be day workers waiting to get into the building,' she said to herself, then she saw a lady opening the doors from the outside with a key. Why would they not be opened from the inside? There were girls sleeping in the building. Soon Pimchan would find out just how things worked in the factory.

She had to report to the office as a new worker and was given a piece of paper to read with her conditions of work, her pay and what amount would be deducted, if she chose to sleep on a flax mat on the factory floor. Many of the young girls working there, like her, had no choice other than to bed down on the floor. The factory doors were locked at eight o'clock at night and reopened at seven o'clock in the morning. This meant the girls could not leave the building once the doors were locked. Pimchan needed the money so had to accept these conditions that had been presented to her. She was then shown to a machine and assigned an assistant for the day to teach her what to do. At the moment they were sewing T-shirts for the local market; these had been cut in another department and brought through for the girls to sew.

Pimchan looked around the factory. It was packed with girls at machines, all sitting close together, but no one took any notice of her; they had their heads down and were busy sewing. She noticed the small windows high up providing very little ventilation and certainly no view for the girls. This confirmed her earlier thoughts. There was an ablution block at the end of the building, which was accessible from the huge sewing room, but the workers were encouraged to use these facilities at breaks only. Having lived in the country, this was like a prison to Pimchan. She did wonder how the girls survived in the humidity in such a closed-up area. She was about to find out! Garment workers were at the bottom of the chain, yet they were the base and the strength of the clothing industry.

After having spent her first week in the factory, Pimchan was just another girl at a machine. Her first night was a nightmare. At the end of the day the girls cooked their rice on their little gas cookers. Very few words were spoken, but this suited Pimchan as she had been brought up in silence and this was part of her make-up. At eight o'clock a lady came around and announced the door was being locked from the outside and would be reopened in the morning, when the day workers arrived for work. When it came to bedtime each girl had a mat to sleep on. The first girls to shower were the lucky ones as they managed to have lukewarm water, but after that the showers were cold, so they were short and sharp. These facilities were substandard. The girls would curl up in their blankets and drop off to sleep. Pimchan was kept awake by young girls sobbing.

Sweatshops were sometimes implicated in human trafficking, or through 'debt bonding' drawing young girls from the uneducated rural poor, who were forced to work to pay off their parents' debt. The garment industry was notoriously cruel to women and young girls. They were the lowest-paid workers in the world and treated badly, as they were expected to work in fire-prone factories where doors were locked in an environmental emergency. They were treated to innumerable injustices because corporations, many based in America, thought they could get away with it. The meaning of sweatshop: contractors 'sweat' profits from the workers.

The older girls or married ones who left at the end of each day were the lucky ones. Pimchan found the confinement suffocating and she feared for her safety if fire swept through the building, as they were on the third floor and the doors were locked from the outside. This was partly to keep the men and boys from the leather factory next door from entering the building, as the girls couldn't let them in. Also, for fear of the theft of garments from the factory. She hoped this wasn't going to be her life for too long; if so, she would crawl further into her shell.

Pimchan was no real beauty, but her beautiful smile lit up her face and her lovely white teeth were definitely her defining features. Unfortunately, her smile was not seen much around the factory for there was very little to smile about. Today she would have to leave the factory after work and go to the markets to buy some more rice and be back before the door was locked. As she walked down the alleyway, a couple of young lads called out to her so she looked around and they came over. They said they were going to the market and she told them that was where she was going, so they walked together. They told her they worked next door at the leather factory, stitching together leather products. They were heading to the market to buy cooked food to eat, but all Pimchan could afford was a bag of rice and some more chillies. They talked for a short time then she realised she had to be back before the door was locked. This didn't happen at the leather factory, they could come and go as they pleased. One of the lads was taken by her smile and asked her when she was going to the market next. She told him it wouldn't be for another week, when her rice ran out, so he said he would look out for her. Pimchan smiled at him, this he picked up as an invitation.

Although she was nearly sixteen, she did not want this to be her life, as she had hoped for a better future. She had often dreamed of meeting a young man so she could escape the web she was caught in, but she was in total ignorance of the consequences that might follow a meeting with the opposite sex. She was wanting to seek a little happiness, something she had not really experienced in her few years of being a teenager.

Another two months had gone by and she was still at her same machine, but she had new girls working either side of her. The girls came and went regularly and each time they seemed to be getting younger. They were from the poorer rural villages and this was a culture shock for them. Pimchan would hear them crying at night as they lay wrapped in their blankets, but, like her, they would soon get used to it. One girl didn't have a gas cooker so Pimchan shared her rice with this young soul. She, like Pimchan, had been sent to work by her parents to pay back debts they had incurred. Sadly, the girls had become slaves to their parents as well as to the bosses of the textile sweat-shops. These factories were mainly owned by overseas companies, and sadly it was the clothing retailers who were the big winners in all this. The workers worked nine hours a day, six days a week. When overseas contracts came in, the girls were paid a little extra per garment.

Lawana, Pimchan's sister, was now working in a textile weaving factory in Bangkok, but it was on the other side of town to where Pimchan worked. Her working conditions were no different to that of her sister, the only difference being she worked alongside men and boys. It was a mixed workforce. The sisters would often meet in the city, as it was cheaper for them both to take a bus and meet in the middle. Not a lot of words passed between them, but just to see each other was a welcome change from the factory machines. They would sit in the park surrounded by the noise of the traffic and the thick city fog, and think of the wide-open spaces back in their little village of Kantharalak. There were only a couple of vehicles in their village; most times the transport was a motorcycle carrying up to four passengers at any one time. Life was lived there as it happened, family and friends lived off each other, they shared, they fought with closed fists, but debts were always repaid … at the children's expense. This, the children seemed to accept, but, really, they had no other option because of their lack of education. Not many doors opened for them, especially as they were girls. But this did not stop them from dreaming of a better life! Dreams cost nothing, they were free, so they could indulge in this pastime as often as their thoughts allowed. It was all they had to look forward to; life offered them very little else.

4

FIVE YEARS ON

LAWANA WAS NOW MARRIED with two children. She had wed a boy who worked alongside her in the textile factory. They had rented a one-bedroom flat in the city, and they were struggling, as now there was only one wage coming in. Pimchan was called upon to help out her sister financially, as well as her parents. Because the flat was small and had only one bedroom, they all slept together on a mattress on the floor. This was all they could afford, but it was inconvenient for a family of four. When Lawana found out she was pregnant with her third child, she was devastated. There was no way they could afford to feed another baby on one wage, as they could barely make ends meet feeding the two little ones they already had. There was no light at the end of the tunnel, even with the help from her sister. And another child in the tiny flat was going to be nigh on impossible, so a decision had to be made. Lawana approached her parents to see if the children could live with them. This would allow her to go back to work and she would send money home for her parents and her children. This was welcomed by her family as it meant they would have access to a little more money other than Pimchan's payments. This would all take place after the baby was born, so in the meantime Pimchan still had to help out both families financially.

Her life had not altered much in five years; she was still at the same machine and had seen many girls come and go at the factory. Many left because they were pregnant, mostly to boys from the leather factory next door. Finally, she had formed a friendship with the young lad she met in the alleyway on her first week of work. He was working to send money home to his family; it was a never-ending cycle for these young teenagers. They were nothing more than cash cows, working to pay off their families' debts. They too had dreams, but they came second, their family came first; dreams came later, in many cases years later. Their friendship was just that, they were friends. Pravat was more outgoing than Pimchan and he probably read more into this friendship than she, as she had never changed, often retreating into periods of silence. All the time she had worked at the factory, her savings were non-existent because of her commitments, first to her parents, then to Lawana.

One day after work, Pimchan walked to the markets to replenish her rice supply as it was running low, and while there she ran into Pravat. A conversation soon started and he asked her if he could buy her something to eat. They walked the markets together and he bought her cooked grasshoppers from a street vendor, which they shared. Before she realised, eight o'clock had slipped by, which meant she was locked out of the factory. What would she do? "Come and stay in my room, then you can go in with the day girls in the morning," said Pravat. Pimchan accepted, as she had nowhere else to go. At the back of the leather factory there was a tall building filled with tiny dormitories. These were for the leather workers, so at least she had somewhere to sleep.

When they arrived, she was surprised at how tiny the room was. In fact, it was just a cubicle, so she had to share a single bed with Pravat. She climbed on the bed fully dressed and turned her back on him. She felt him lying close to her; no one had ever been this close to her, ever! She was tired and drifted off to sleep. Then she was woken by hands touching her body inside her clothes. She sat up and there was Pravat totally naked with his hands inside her knickers. She was startled, this had never happened before. Why was he touching her? This was her body. She started to cry. Suddenly he pushed her down and climbed on top of her while pulling down her knickers, then he put his hand over her mouth, so no one could hear her. She felt him moving up and down on her, then there was pain. Pimchan lay there petrified, fearing for her life. What was he going to do next? Instead, he just rolled off her and dropped off to sleep. She was thankful nothing else happened. She quietly sobbed as she didn't understand what had taken place. She pulled up her knickers and tucked her dress between her legs, then went off to sleep.

The next morning, she woke to see several lads standing at the end of the bed staring at them and laughing. "Beggar off!" Pravat told them. When they left, he leaned over and kissed Pimchan. She couldn't understand why he had hurt her last night then kissed her this morning, perhaps he did like her? She climbed off the bed and made her way down the alley to where the girls were waiting for the factory doors to open. As they were being opened, she rushed past the girls and went straight to the bathroom and bathed herself. All day she sewed away at her machine in a daze, trying to work out what last night was all about, as she had no idea. Because of her silent nature she had never asked questions. Her mother never talked to her about what happened between a man and a woman, so she was oblivious as to what had taken place.

Several days came and went and Pimchan was too frightened to venture outside the factory, as she didn't want to see Pravat any time soon. When Sunday arrived, she mingled with a group of girls as they left the building, then ran to the bus stop. She was going to visit Lawana, perhaps she could ask her what had happened. The bus was packed so she had to stand until someone got off, then she was able to sit down, as it was going to take her forty-five minutes to reach her destination. When she arrived at her stop, she got off the bus and ran down the hill to Lawana's flat. It was an overcast smoggy day, and they would not be taking the children out today. It would be healthier for them to stay indoors.

Pimchan knocked at the door waiting to hear her

sister's voice before entering. As she went into the flat, the children were crying and Lawana was sitting in a chair with her head in her hands. She was due to give birth any day and it had all got on top of her. Her husband couldn't afford to take time off work to look after the children while she was in hospital. What were they going to do? "I will take some of my holidays and come and look after the children," volunteered Pimchan. "Will you do that for me, my sister?" asked Lawana. They arranged it there and then so there would be no more worries as to what would happen to the children. Lawana's husband would ring Pimchan at the factory when she went into labour, then she would catch the bus over straight away. She would have to sleep on the lounge floor, due to the lack of room in the flat.

Now it was time to ask Lawana why this strange thing had happened to her while she lay in Pravat's bed. She asked why he had climbed on top of her and hurt her then went to sleep, but in the morning, he had kissed her. Poor Lawana, she didn't know what to say. "Has no one told you about sex?" she asked. "Pravat had sex with you, that is what happens when two people like each other. It hurts the first time but then it gets better. Did you not know what was happening? Oh Pimchan, someone should have told you, you are twenty years of age." "Was that okay for him to do that to me? I was frightened for my life," she said. "Yes, that is perfectly natural for a man to want to bed a woman, but they usually ask. Just be careful, as that is how you get pregnant. Look at me, don't let this happen to you, Pimchan, it is such a worry. I am going to have to part with my children and let mother and father bring them up so I can go back to work, otherwise we couldn't survive. This is not the life I dreamed of," she said with a sob. The two sisters cried in each other's arms. Would their dreams come anywhere near what they wanted in their hearts?

Pimchan was working at her machine when she received the call that Lawana was in labour. Only emergency calls were allowed through in working hours. She wasn't sure how many days she would be away but the lady boss knew her story. She packed her things and ran to the bus stop. When she arrived at Lawana's flat, a taxi was waiting to take her to the hospital, as her pains were getting closer together. Her husband had just arrived so he went in the taxi with Lawana, as he had been allowed to take the afternoon off. Pimchan lifted the pushchair out the door and put the youngest child in, as it was a lovely day so they were going to the park. It was easier to entertain the children at the park rather than in the tiny flat.

She sat and watched the children playing, wondering if her life was going to be a replica of her sister's or if, in fact, she was ever going to leave the sweatshop. In the five years she had worked there, her father's debt had been paid off, but how long was that going to last? she asked herself. But she would have to keep helping Lawana, as they could not manage on a single wage.

She didn't feel so bad now that she knew what Pravat had done was perfectly natural. Did he like her? She wouldn't be frightened next time. "Pimchan, come and play with us!" yelled two little voices, taking her thoughts away from him. She walked over and pushed the children on the swings. They had a nice afternoon together, now it was time to go back to the flat.

When Lawana's husband came home later in the night, he told her that they had another little boy. Now their family consisted of a girl and two boys. Everything had gone well, so it was thought that Lawana would be home in two days. Pimchan would stay on for a couple of days, taking the children to the park so Lawana could get some rest. Not much in the way of conversation passed between Lawana's husband and Pimchan, but this didn't worry him, as he knew of her silent ways, he had experienced them before. At first, he thought there was something wrong with her, but now he knew otherwise. He went to his bedroom and tucked up on the mattress with his children. She curled up in her blanket on the lounge floor and went to sleep.

The next morning, he was up early and away to work before she surfaced, although she had heard him in the kitchenette. The children were still asleep so she just lay there and her mind drifted back to Pravat. She wondered if he was waiting for her outside the factory in the alleyway. She knew very little about him, other than he was working to send money home to his parents. Their situations were similar, but then, so were those of most of the girls at the sweatshop. They were working to prop up their families, or repay their parents' debt. No wonder very few words passed from one girl to the next, they were like robots working at machines. The only bright side was meeting the lads from the leather factory. Pimchan had noticed a strange machine on the wall in the bathroom at the factory but she never asked what it was, although she had noticed girls removing items and they didn't seem to have to pay for them. Suddenly her daydreaming came to an end because there were two little children standing by the door.

She jumped up and dressed, as it was time to feed them, they were hungry. The kitchenette was small, with a sink, a small bench and two gas hobs. There were three cupboards and a small fridge in the corner. They ate in the lounge as there was no room for a table and chairs. The flat was very small but this was all they could afford, in fact most flats were this size in the city, They were built to accommodate working couples, not families. Pimchan rang her family to tell them that Lawana had had a baby boy. They told her Chetak had finished his time at the temple and was now working in an office in Bangkok. He had met a girl whose family was quite well off. Because of his time as a novice monk he had learnt well, so was able to get an office job. But he was not forthcoming with any money to help his family. This was left to the girls, as their standing did not come near that of their brother. Being the eldest and the only son, nothing was expected from him by his parents.

Today was a warm, sunny day, too good to stay inside, so Pimchan decided to take the children to a nearby temple, as she hadn't been for a long time. She would light a candle and say some prayers. As she was walking up the steps to the entrance, she was stopped by a group of tourists wanting to ask questions about the temple. As Pimchan had learnt a little English at school she was able to communicate with them but with much difficulty, and because of her shyness she was not able to look at them directly. She hung her head; this was the inferior feeling of the rural poor. She was able to tell them a little about the temple and they showed their gratitude by giving her money. This was not expected and she felt very humble.

The tourists were happy to give this poor mother money to help feed her children! She decided to buy Lawana some perfume, perhaps she would feel a little better about herself after having the baby. There was a little money left over, so Pimchan bought some pork for that night's meal. She would cook larb moo, a stir-fry dish with pork, lime juice, fish sauce and grain-roasted rice with spring onions, mint and coriander. This was a popular Thai dish.

That night as she lay on the lounge floor, her thoughts went back to the tourists at the temple and the money she had been given. Perhaps if she learnt English she could go to the temple and help more tourists and be paid. This was a thought that flashed through her mind, but then silence reigned and all previous thoughts disappeared as quickly as they arrived. This was a problem for Pimchan; she had no confidence to carry anything through to fruition. There had been very little guidance in her life from her parents, other than work and survival.

Today Lawana was bringing her baby home so she had to get a taxi from the hospital. This was another expense that they couldn't afford so Pimchan paid the driver and lifted out Lawana's bag. The baby was all wrapped up until they entered the flat, then it was time to let everyone see the new arrival. The baby was oblivious to all around him, he just kept on sleeping even when kisses were bestowed on him. Lawana put him in the bedroom in his little canvas crib on the mattress. Now there would be five sharing it, but this would just be for a short time. When she stopped breast-feeding, they would take the children to the parents until they could afford to live as a family again, then they would bring them home. This would be in the lap of the gods.

Pimchan took the children to the park again today so her sister could have bonding time with her new baby and hopefully manage time for a little rest. Tonight, she would cook a traditional dinner of rice with a green papaya salad. Lawana's husband did not arrive home until very late, as he was kept back at work to finish an urgent order that had to be dispatched that night. He ate his dinner and went straight to bed as he was tired. During the night Pimchan heard the baby crying. The husband was upset as he needed his sleep — he had work the next day — but he could not escape, there was nowhere to go. This was far from an ideal set-up, but their choices were indeed very limited. This was their life, one from which there was no escaping; it was called merely existing! Pimchan felt deeply for her sister. 'Please do not let this be my life,' she whispered to herself.

It was back to work at the sweatshop, head down and sewing in silence. Pimchan was trying to work out whose life was worth less, hers or her sister's. She wondered how life was measured, was she ever going to find out? Was there a ray of hope on the horizon, or was the horizon beyond her reach? At this place in time, there was no answer — no horizon and almost no hope!

Her bag of rice was empty again so it was time for a trip to the market. As she was leaving the building someone waved to her, it was Pravat. He had been looking out for her. "I have been waiting for you, where have you been?" he asked. Pimchan could hardly look at him remembering what had happened in his bed. "Don't you like me?" he asked. She kept her head down not knowing what to say. She was dreading this moment, what was she meant to say? She slowly lifted her head and flashed him one of her beautiful smiles. This made him feel as if this was, perhaps, a yes? He stayed with her while she bought her bag of rice, then they walked back in silence. When they reached the alleyway, Pravat took Pimchan's hand and asked, "Do you want to come to my bed tonight?" She shook her head, she was frightened. "Come tomorrow night?" he asked. She nodded then opened the factory door and disappeared inside. What a strange girl, Pravat thought to himself, but he secretly liked her when she smiled.

That night as she lay on her mat wrapped up snug in her blanket, she wondered what would happen in Pravat's bed tomorrow night. Lawana had told her when two people liked each other it was natural for things to happen. She hadn't met many lads, she had certainly not had one wanting to touch her before, but if this was natural, then it was okay. She was secretly pleased that he liked her, she just didn't know how to handle these personal situations, it was all foreign to her. She had never had to express her feelings to anyone, in fact she didn't know she had any until now, when she thought of Pravat.

Another work day had come to an end. Pimchan showered and put on a clean dress and brushed her thick black hair. As she walked out the factory door Pravat was waiting for her. He smiled, as he wasn't sure if she would come tonight. "Come to the market with me and we will get something to eat?" he asked of her. As they walked to the market, she felt Pravat take her hand. She liked this; he must really like me, she thought. He bought her some fried rice and bamboo worms, her favourite, from a street vendor, then he bought himself fried grasshoppers with rice.

Tonight, there was no hurry to rush back before eight o'clock because she was staying with Pravat in his bed. They walked around the market looking at the stalls, still holding hands. Pimchan started to feel a warmth, which was a new feeling for her, as she had never held a lad's hand before. They made their way back to his dormitory and climbed onto his bed. "Do you like me, Pimchan?" he asked her. "I think so," she answered with a shy smile. He leaned over and kissed her. She lay down and pulled the blanket over her, waiting for something to happen. Pravat undressed and climbed on the bed beside her. He moved close and put his hands under the blanket and she felt him moving them over her body. He stopped at her knickers and pulled them down. He rolled her on her back and climbed on top of her, fondling her breasts and kissing her bare skin. She liked this. He must really like me, she kept thinking to herself, and with this thought she relaxed. Then something happened; it didn't hurt this time, it was different, she liked this feeling. He was moving up and down on her and she felt her hands reaching up to him pulling him down on her. Then she let out a squeal, and with that she felt his hand cover her mouth, he didn't want the other lads to come running. He rolled off her. "Did you like that?" She nodded and smiled to let him know that she did.

He lay with his arms around her and they drifted off to sleep. In the morning when she woke Pravat was already dressed and was talking to several boys at the door. They waved to Pimchan and she waited until they were gone before she climbed out of bed. She was still half-dressed so straightened up her clothes, but her knickers were missing. She searched for them and found them at the end of the bed. She pulled them on and smiled as she thought of last night. As she passed Pravat she said, "Thank you." He knew then she would be back, many times he hoped.

5

THE DOWRY

Pimchan's brother, Chetak, had taken his courtship to another level and had asked his girl to marry him. But before this could happen there was the talk of a dowry. Although her family's wealth was far more than that of Chetak's family, he was expected to pay her family a dowry to take their daughter away. He had saved very little money so went to his family asking them to put up the dowry. They owned their own home, humble as it was, and the piece of land surrounding it. Because Chetak was the eldest child and the only son, he expected his family to provide this for him. The only way for them to do this was to sell their home and land, leaving them nowhere to live, but this is what was about to happen. One of his father's brothers offered to build an iron lean-to onto the side of his home for them to live under.

When the home sold, the money was given to Chetak to pay the dowry to the bride's parents, then the marriage could take place. Now Pimchan's parents were virtually homeless, so she was expected to send more money home for them. They would live in the lean-to until they could get enough money together to build again. One of the uncles owned a little block of land where they could build their new home. Her father was offered work helping a German landowner plant a block of lancewood trees. This would keep him off the alcohol, and if he managed this, he could afford to buy concrete bricks to start the new house. It would be a basic dwelling with block walls and a roof. The floor would be earthen and all the cooking would be done outside of the build. A large cauldron would be set up over an open fire, as no cooking would be allowed inside the shelter as it was solely for sleeping.

This would be one big room where everyone slept on bamboo mats. There was some urgency to get the dwelling finished, as Lawana's children were nearly due to begin life with the grandparents. Once again, the lending cycle had begun as the father borrowed money from his siblings to finish the build, but it was only a loan and would have to be paid back … by whom?

Chetak was now married but he was never forthcoming with any money to support his parents. This was just accepted as such. He broke the news that his wife was pregnant so was no longer able to work. Once again, the poverty cycle was starting; it just seemed to flow on from one generation to the next. Although he had a reasonable paying office job, he lived in a different world to that of his family. His wants far exceeded those of his parents, simply because he could afford them. But conveniently he forgot what his family had sacrificed for him; it was the daughters who were expected to work and pay everything back.

When it was time for the grandchildren to arrive, there would be money coming from Lawana as she was expected to keep her parents as well as her children. She had no other option, but this didn't exempt Pimchan from any of the family responsibilities, as she was working to pay off the new loan her father had borrowed from his siblings.

6

INNOCENCE CAN BE BITTER

SIX MONTHS HAD PASSED and Lawana had taken the children to her parents' place, as it was nigh on possible for them to keep living in the cramp conditions at the tiny flat. Money had become a huge worry, there just wasn't enough for them to survive. She was back at her factory job working alongside her husband, where they had first met. It had been sad for her to leave her children behind, but she told herself it would not be for long, as something better would come along! She had a vision!

Pimchan had been visiting Pravat often and sharing his bed, even enjoying their times together. She knew how warm it felt in his arms and when he took her, she willingly responded. He even had claw marks on his back to prove this. That was until one day while working at her machine she suddenly started feeling sick. This went on for a month and she began to worry. She had told no one. One day while visiting Lawana, Pimchan mentioned this to her, and she knew straight away what was wrong with her sister. "Pimchan, you are pregnant. Did you not use anything to prevent this from happening?" "What do you mean?" she asked. "Did Pravat not use a condom?" "I don't know," answered Pimchan. Her sister told her she would have to visit a doctor. Pimchan started to cry; she wasn't ready to have a family, she wasn't even married. What would Pravat say when she told him? But even worse, what would she do? Where would she go? She couldn't go home, there wouldn't be enough room for her and a baby, and who would pay off her father's debt? All these thoughts flashed through her mind; her brain was in meltdown.

By the time Pimchan took the time off work to visit the doctor, her belly was starting to swell. She hadn't been to visit Pravat for nearly a month, as she wanted to hear what the doctor had to say. He told her straight, "You are four months pregnant, Pimchan." She didn't want to hear these words, but now there was no escape as the doctor had told her the cold hard truth. Now she would have to tell Pravat. Would he want to stay with her? she wondered.

That night when she went to his dormitory, he was so pleased to see her, as he was wondering why she hadn't been to share his bed. He asked her to get under the blanket, and he turned his back and got undressed. When he turned around Pimchan was just standing there, she hadn't climbed onto the bed. Why wasn't she ready for him? He was so excited. "Pravat, I am having a baby, our baby," she told him. He looked at her in disbelief. "I went to the doctor today and he told me I am four months pregnant. What are we going to do?" Poor Pravat, his mind was engaged on other things. All he wanted was to have sex with Pimchan. He hadn't thought of the consequences. To him it was all just fun, he enjoyed sex, if not with Pimchan it would have been with someone else. What was going to happen? The two of them had not thought to the future, but now, it was there before them.

He tried to coax her to get under the blanket with him, then it would all be forgotten for a little while, but she wanted to deal with it right now. "I will speak to my parents and see what they have to say, perhaps they will let you live with them," he told her. "But I have never met your parents," and with this she started to cry. He put his arms around her and lifted her onto his bed and pulled up the blanket. His answer to all this was to have sex, so off came her knickers. This showed how irresponsible he was. He had not faced his responsibilities, he had just put them aside. Pimchan stayed the night with him, as she didn't want to be alone with these frightening thoughts!

Pimchan was in her seventh month of pregnancy and was still working at the factory. Pravat had taken her home to meet his parents, who lived in their own little house in a small village. They didn't seem to be as poor as her family, but why was he sending money home? she wondered. Because of this they agreed she could live with them so Pravat could keep working, but they told them they had to marry, so this they did. There was no talk of a dowry as she hadn't told her family yet of her pregnancy. She only had one week left at the sweatshop before moving in with her in-laws. This meant she would only see Pravat on a Sunday. She was sad about this but there were no other choices … this was it!

The time had come for her to ring her family and tell them her predicament and that there would be no more money forthcoming, as she was finishing work. They were sad for Pimchan, but life was just as it happened. She would have to accept her fate and cope as best she could, as they could do nothing to help. Because of their poverty-filled lives, whatever happened to the children was of their own doing, their own choice, so it was up to them to fend for themselves. This was the Thai way of life and it was passing down to the next generation. There was no expression of love or happiness; perhaps if it was there, it was hidden, as seen in Pimchan. Silence was a big part of her life and for her to show her feelings was rare indeed. Would she be able to keep Pravat happy, as he was more outgoing …? Only time would tell!

The time had nearly arrived for Pimchan to give birth. She had moved in with her in-laws but she was unhappy with only seeing Pravat each Sunday. She didn't speak much with his parents as she felt a stranger in their house. She did, however, find a book on English, so she spent most of her time trying to teach herself how to write and speak a little of the English language. Perhaps this might come in handy one day, as she had many dreams of a better life.

Pravat had asked for a week off work when the baby was born so he could help Pimchan. She went into labour in the early hours of the morning, but was afraid to wake her in-laws, so she waited until she heard them moving around the house before she called to them. They rang for a cab to take her to the hospital, then they contacted Pravat. She had not spoken to anyone about the birth process so did not know what to expect. She went into the final stages of labour and suffered without uttering a word. The staff were amazed, they could not believe this girl; this was her first baby and through all her pain, she suffered in silence. When the baby was born, she drifted off to sleep.

Later she was woken and her baby was brought in for her to feed. The nursing staff had to show her what to do. Although she had seen her sister, Lawana, breast-feeding her baby, she knew little; now she was doing the same. She looked at her little boy and wondered what Pravat would think. Later in the day when he arrived, he kissed Pimchan and asked if he could see his son. The nurse brought in the baby for him to hold, and he seemed to be happy with him. She watched him talking to their baby, then she drifted off to sleep. She was woken by screams; it was dark and she was on her own. Why would anyone be screaming? she wondered. It was frightening. It went on most of the night and people seemed to be rushing everywhere. Pimchan curled up under her sheet trying to block out the noise, as it took her back to the sweatshop and the young girls sobbing at night. She seemed to be in places where girls were sad, then she looked at her own life … it was sad too!

The next day Pravat came to visit Pimchan and to hold his baby boy. She was happy that he liked his baby, and to see him cuddling him and giving him kisses made her happy. "I have thought of a name for our little boy. I will call him Chai," he said. Pimchan hadn't thought about a name so agreed with her husband. She sat in silence watching Pravat talking away to his son, as he seemed to be more interested in the baby than her. Tomorrow she was allowed to go home, so they made arrangements for him to come and pick them up and take them home to his parents' house.

She wasn't looking forward to going back to her in-laws. Would the baby cry and keep them awake at night? This was a big worry. But Pravat would be there with her for the next four nights. He kissed her goodbye when he left; she would be home with him after one more sleep. The night was long as she was kept awake by more screams. She couldn't understand why this was happening, but not everyone was a silent sufferer like herself. She kept her feelings and her pain hidden in her heart so no one knew from the outside what she was thinking or indeed if she was suffering. This was her lot to bear.

Pravat had arrived to pick up his family. The cab waited until they were ready, then took them home. He nursed Chai, who chose to sleep all the way. Pimchan sat quietly; she was having one of her silent periods of withdrawal, blocking out the world around her. Pravat had to shake her to awaken her from her daydream when they pulled up outside his parents' home. He took his baby in to show him off to his parents, he was so proud. They took turns at holding Chai. Poor Pimchan was the forgotten one, although she had done the suffering. She had never seen such love bestowed on a child before, this was indeed foreign to her. At last her in-laws acknowledged her and smiled at her achievement. The next four days passed quickly and Pravat was a great help with baby Chai, he showed him so much love. Pimchan didn't seem to be as emotional from an outside prospective, but what was going on inside, sadly was hidden from all. She was upset to have to say goodbye to her husband, as she wouldn't see him until Sunday.

The next year came and went and Pimchan was still living with her in-laws. She and Pravat had managed to save a little money. She wanted them to move out and into a flat of their own, near his workplace, so he could be home each night. She had become attached to him. There was never any mention of love between them, this was not a loving relationship. As long as Pimchan provided him with sex he was happy, but he did love his son. They were forced together by the pregnancy and he had stood by her. Now they knew they had to use preventatives when sleeping together so there would be no more mistakes. Pimchan kept on his back about finding a flat, so he was keeping his eye out for one which they could afford.

Today they were moving into their own apartment in a

large housing block. Pravat had found a one-bedroom apartment, which was all they needed at the moment as their son would share the bedroom with them. They were used to this, as they had to share a bedroom when living with his parents. This was the norm for most households with young families in the city, as this was all they could afford. Pravat bought a bed for him and Pimchan, as they had slept in a bed while at his parents' house. He liked to have her close, as it was easier for him to satisfy his wants.

Pimchan was happy; this was the first time in her life she had her independence and full responsibility for a place of her own. Perhaps this is what she needed to bring her out of her silent periods. But they soon learnt that by the time the rent was paid and they had to live on only one wage, there were no luxuries. It was back to a life of poverty and struggle. Chai was now walking, so Pimchan would take him to the park where he could toddle off in the large parklands.

One day she decided to take him to the temple, as she hadn't been for a long time. She thought back to the last time she visited and what had transpired — she had helped some foreigners and was paid for her knowledge. Today she hoped she would have the same luck, as now she knew more English words. As she climbed the steps and approached the entrance, a group of tourists asked her what was expected of them when they entered the temple. She explained that they had to cover their bare legs and not to make bodily contact with the monks, as this was forbidden. The women purchased saris and wrapped them around their waists. "I take you in, you follow what I do," Pimchan told them. For this they were very grateful and walked behind her, following her every move, so as not to offend the gods. She didn't have to speak to them, as silence was observed in the temple.

As they were leaving, they took notes out of their pockets and gave them to Pimchan for her help. She felt guilty taking money outside the temple as it was a sacred place of worship, but she was in need of a little extra. She waited until she was back at the apartment before she counted the notes. It was a lot of money, more than what she could have earned for two weeks of work at the sweat-shop. Pravat would be pleased with her. When he came home that night and was told about the money, he was very happy, but where did she get it from? Pimchan had some explaining to do. Once this was all sorted out, he asked her to get under the blanket and in their excitement, they forgot all about safety precautions.

Nine months later Pimchan was in the hospital again, giving birth to their baby daughter. Pravat didn't want to name the baby. He told her to choose a name, so she chose Mali. He didn't show much interest in this new baby because she was a girl. He had taken two weeks off work to be home to look after Chai while Pimchan gave birth. When she brought Mali home, the bedroom became crowded as the baby had to share a mattress on the floor with Chai. Baby Mali cried a lot at night, disturbing the peace and upsetting Chai who became grumpy, so Pravat insisted that he lay in their bed between them. This was okay while Pimchan was recovering from the birth but when he wanted to have sex it was not ideal, as Chai refused to go back to sleeping on the mattress, he wanted to be by his father. As the months came and went, Pimchan noticed that Pravat seemed less interested in her and had very little to do with Mali. He would take Chai to the park on a Sunday but never asked to take Mali with them.

7

PRAVAT'S WANDERING EYE

WHILE AT TIIE market one day during his lunch break, Pravat's eye was taken by a happy bubbly young girl who seemed to have her group of friends captivated. They were gathering around her listening intently to what she was saying, then roars of laughter would ring out. He stood and looked at her, then something happened to him that he had never felt before: his heart started beating faster and he became flustered. Who was this stranger? He waited until they made a move and watched in which direction they were heading. Pravat decided to follow them, staying behind so he wasn't noticed, and was surprised to see they were heading in the direction of the sweatshop. When they reached the alleyway, they turned down and disappeared through the sweatshop door. So now he knew where she worked.

The next day in his lunch break he waited in the alleyway hoping to catch a glance of this happy soul, but sadly she was not to be seen. He felt heartbroken. All week he stood in the alleyway during his lunch break but alas to no avail. As he lay in bed at night beside Pimchan, he dreamed of this mystery girl, thus not wanting to bed Pimchan any more.

On Sunday he told Pimchan he was meeting up with some of his work friends, so he would be away for the day. She was not at all happy as this was his only day off work. He walked to the market hoping to see this happy young girl, but where to start? he asked himself. As he wondered through the crowds, there she was, on her own. He quickly made his way over to where he saw her, only to find her trying to barter with a stall vendor over a scarf. She only had a certain amount of money but the vendor would not budge on her price. She was devastated as she had fallen in love with the scarf and just had to have it, but was shy of a few baht. "Excuse me, I will pay the difference," offered Pravat. The young girl accepted his kind gesture so the sale went through. As soon as the scarf was in her hands, she put it over her head making her look more mysterious, thus causing the strangest feelings to take over Pravat's body.

What was wrong? he asked himself. Then she looked him straight in the eye and thanked him. With this a conversation began between them and he learnt she was no different to most of the other sweatshop girls — she was there because her parents had bonded her to a debtor. Therefore, she had to pay off the debt. But why was she so happy? She could still laugh and seemed very popular with the other girls. He was bewildered that she oozed such happiness, he had never felt this warmth in his body for anyone. Why now?

They walked back to the factory together both laughing as she told him about the stories she had read from books. That was why she had to have the scarf, she wanted to become the mysterious lady she had read about last night. The scarf was the camouflage for what lay beneath. Pravat was intrigued. She portrayed an outward persona of one who believed in a happy-ever-after. She was his fairy-tale princess. He just had to meet her again. "You make me feel happy inside, can we meet again?" he asked. He explained he worked next door at the leather factory. "Can I meet you at your lunch break tomorrow, here in the alley?" She agreed, as he seemed to like her stories.

Pravat was happy. He couldn't wait until tomorrow, but it seemed a long way off. Now he had to go home to Pimchan and the children, to a home where there was very little laughter. Chai brought him joy but he didn't have the same feeling for Mali. He never really loved Pimchan. They were both lonely and he had taken advantage of her loneliness by bedding her for sex. Sadly there were consequences, but he didn't abandon her. But now he was realising that he wanted more from life, this being brought to the fore by having set eyes on the mystery girl. She was so full of life, she made him laugh, and now he realised this was missing from his life. Pimchan's silent periods annoyed him. He had hoped they would disappear but no, they still prevailed, but why? He tried his best to make her happy, but it made no difference. Was he ready for a change? He couldn't wait until lunch break tomorrow!

Time seemed to be on a go-slow at the leather factory this morning as Pravat watched the hands moving. They were just ticking slowly taking their time. Couldn't they see he had an important appointment? As soon as the lunch gong rang, he was the first out the door, then he ran along the alleyway to wait at the door of the sweatshop. His heart was racing, he just had to see her again. As the sweatshop door opened, there she was, wearing her scarf and talking to a group of girls. Pravat waved to her and she left the girls and came over to him. "I like you with the scarf on, it suits you," he said. "This is my sophisticated look," she laughingly told Pravat. "I like pretending I'm someone from my storybooks. Today I am very rich, so I can be happy because I can have whatever I want." He was bewildered. How could a storybook make someone so happy? He asked if he could buy her some lunch, but she refused.

They continued talking and she told him stories making him laugh. She was such a happy soul. He wanted to tell her how he felt but it was too soon. He moved closer to her and gently touched her hand to get a feeling to see if she was interested. She didn't withdraw her hand and he saw her blush. Was this telling him she liked him? "What is your name?" Pravat asked. "I am Kannika, a poor girl from a poor home, but I can be happy by reading books." He couldn't deny this, she was like a breath of fresh air. "How old are you?" She told him she was fifteen. Suddenly the gong rang out and it was time to go back to work. "Can I meet you again tomorrow, Kannika?" he asked. "Yes," she said with a smile, then headed back through the door into the sweatshop.

Three weeks had passed and Pravat and Kannika met each lunch break, both enjoying each other's company. He had fallen in love with her — he knew it was love because he was so happy and he missed her every minute they were apart. He had never felt like this before. He hadn't had sex with Pimchan since he met Kannika, he was not interested in her any more.

8

PIMCHAN'S LIFE CHANGE

MALI WAS NOW a year old and Chai was nearly three. She noticed Pravat was distancing himself from her, he didn't even want to have sex with her. He was an outgoing young man but she was different to him, she receded into her inner self unable to express her feelings, thus from the outside she always seemed unhappy. But she was happy within at times, not that anyone would have known!

One day out of the blue, Pravat told Pimchan she had to leave the apartment with her daughter as he didn't want to live with her any more. She had to leave on Sunday. He accused her of having an affair, citing that Mali was not his daughter. She cried as this was not true. Where would she go? There was only one place, and that was back with her parents. But Lawana's three children were still living with their grandparents. How would they all manage? This meant she had to leave her son, as Pravat said he had to stay with him. Pimchan had no other option but to leave on Sunday and take Mali with her.

She had only enough money for their bus fare to her parents' home. Today was Saturday, her last day together with her two children. She needed some money, she couldn't go home empty-handed, so she decided to take the children to the temple. Perhaps she could make some money? She did not like doing this, as she thought it was wrong to earn money from a place of worship, but she was desperate. What else could she do? She prayed there would be foreigners needing help. She made her way to the temple with the children and left the pram at the bottom of the steps. As she reached the top, she was exhausted as she had Mali in her arms, so she sat down to rest.

While she was sitting there a group of foreigners came by and asked if she knew where they could find a guide. "I can help," Pimchan said. "Follow me, I will show you what to do." They felt sorry for this poor young Asian mother so they followed her. As they went into the temple, they watched what Pimchan did. They wanted to experience the calm inside the temple without offending the gods, and to know they could do this brought them great joy. It was all part of their Thailand experience.

As they all came down the steps together, the foreigners asked Pimchan if she could tell them a little about her life. She started to cry, as her life was now worth nothing. What could she tell them? They asked why she was crying, so she told them her plight. "But your husband, does he not have to support you and your daughter?" they asked. She told them, "In Thailand we are so poor there is no money, we live from one pay to the next. When our husband does not want us, we have to go." "Where are you going to live?" they asked. "I have to go home to my parents with my daughter, I have nowhere else to go," she sobbed. These strangers were horrified that this was allowed to happen in this day and age. Who would do this, especially to separate their children? But they did not understand the poverty these people had to endure. A girl's life was nowhere as important as that of the male gender. This was the life they were dealt. It was totally different to the Western world; it was only when the two cultures collided that the cold hard facts emerged.

With this the foreigners all banded together and took money from their pockets and purses and gave it to Pimchan. They wished they could do more for her, but the money would certainly be of help. She bowed to them and thanked them. They wished her well and left feeling very sad for this young mother. She put Mali in the pram and they went to a nearby park where she let the kids play on the grass while she counted the money. It would have taken Pimchan six months of work at the sweatshop to earn this amount of money. Should she give some to Pravat? she wondered, but the stark realisation that he had told her to leave soon changed her way of thinking. She looked at Chai and started to cry. Would she ever see him again?

Tomorrow was Sunday, the day she had to leave, as it was Pravat's day off. He would take Chai to live with his parents during the week and he would pick him up each

Sunday so he could spend time with him. It was barbaric to think he would separate a child from his mother, to give to his parents to bring up, but that's the way it was. Pimchan had no say. She knew she would miss Pravat, but he didn't want her any more. She cried as she said goodbye to Chai. Was this their final goodbye?

Today Pimchan and Mali were on the bus to Kantharalak. She couldn't hide her tears as she thought of leaving Chai and even Pravat, as she had grown to like him. How were they going to live in her parents' shelter with everyone else, as it was only one room? But she had no other choice. She would have to hide her money from her father and use it very sparingly, because when it ran out, she would have to go back to work. What of Mali? The cycle had gone full circle and soon she was going to end up back at the sweat-shirt factory, supporting her daughter and her parents.

They arrived safely. It had been a long day and darkness was setting in so it was time for everyone to nestle down for the night. All the mats were laid out on the floor. Very few words had been spoken and fewer questions were asked, allowing Pimchan to slip back into her silent zone. Nothing had changed much since she left. She fed Mali and lay on her mat with her in her arms and wept silently for Chai and Pravat. Just because she couldn't express her feelings didn't mean she didn't have any; she couldn't get them out, they were locked inside her body.

The next morning Pimchan wrapped Mali in a sarong and tied her to her back, as she was taking her on her first food-gathering outing with her grandmother. Off they set with their basket and pole to find their food source for the day. Now there were extra mouths to feed, a total of seven in all. Pimchan's mother was a sad soul. Her position had always been that of the family food-gatherer, otherwise there would have been nothing to eat. The father was the child-minder when he was not at the temple with the monks drying out. Their voices were rarely heard, it was only Lawana's children that brought life to their home. Today they were going to catch some fish with the long pole. Pimchan caught some grasshoppers and tied them to a line which was tied on to the pole, then they let the hook dangle in the water. It wasn't long before they had enough fish for the night meal and a little extra to put in the monks' offering bowls tomorrow morning. Today all the monks received was grains of rice, as Pimchan had eaten what was put aside for them, as no one had expected her home.

It didn't take Pimchan long to slot back into her old way of life. Little Mali was walking everywhere and Lawana's children loved her. They found an old cart and would put her in and tow her everywhere. Life was so simple. She had been very frugal with her money but it was going to run out soon. Two of Lawana's children walked to school each day, as she and her husband sent money for them to attend school. Pimchan's father was the one who disciplined the children. He would pick Mali up and cuddle her. She was the youngest child and he was forming a bond with her, so Pimchan knew that when time came for her to leave to find work, Mali would be cared for.

9

BACK AT THE SWEATSHOP

TODAY PIMCHAN WAS on her way back to the bustling city of Bangkok. She had begged Pravat to let her stay with him in his flat until she found work, and this would give her a chance to see Chai again. He agreed for her to stay with him. Perhaps he might want her back. Was he missing her? she wondered, with hope in her heart. When she arrived at the flat, she was anxious to see her son. Two years had passed, would he have changed? When she saw him, she could not believe how he had grown, but he just stood and stared at Pimchan. She fought back her tears. "Do you remember me, Chai,? I am your mother." Chai just looked at her, like he would look at a stranger.

His life was now centred around his grandparents, his father and his father's new girlfriend; these were the people he knew, they were all part of his life. No one had talked about his mother so she was a forgotten soul. Suddenly a young girl appeared from the bedroom. "This is my new love, Kannika. We are very happy, we are in love," Pravat told Pimchan. Poor Pimchan, if she had thought there was renewed hope for her and Pravat, that was quickly quashed. She was shocked, she had never heard him mention love before. Not once was this word mentioned while they lived together; perhaps he never really loved her?

Pimchan wanted out of the flat, she needed time to come to terms with what she was confronted with. She asked Pravat if she could take Chai to the park so she could have him to herself. He agreed, as it would give him and Kannika time on their own. As they walked to the park together, it was in silence. Chai was wary of this stranger who said she was his mother. When they found a seat Pimchan asked him to sit with her. "Do you not remember me, Chai?" she asked, hoping there would be some recognition of her. "No," he answered. "Do you know you have a sister? She is two years old," but still he looked blankly at her. Then he asked, "What is her name?" "She is called Mali." "Why isn't she living with me?" he asked.

Pimchan couldn't find the right words to say to him. A silence passed, then she answered. "Mali is living with her grandparents like you live with yours." This is where the conversation finished. Chai left and ran off to the playground. She sat and watched him with tears in her eyes. It was then she realised she was no longer part of his life. But this was life, it was one of acceptance and survival and one of goodbyes. On their way back to the flat she asked him if he was happy and he told her he was. This was all she could hope for. While they sat and had dinner together, Pimchan felt sad. She could see the happiness in Pravat's eyes as they never left Kannika.

Pravat didn't have to take Chai back to his parents' place tonight because Pimchan could take him back tomorrow, and this meant he could have an extra night with his father. They sat and talked together. Pimchan was just a bystander. At bedtime Chai and Pimchan lay on the mattress next to Pravat's bed. During the night she could hear giggles coming from the bed beside her and she knew they were having sex. She felt hurt, that was what she and Pravat used to do in that bed.

When she woke in the morning she lay on the mattress until Pravat and Kannika left for work. Chai was still asleep. She dressed and when Chai woke, she cooked rice for them both, which they ate in silence. Because she had very little money, she could not afford to get a cab so she walked Chai back to his grandparents. It was a long way and she wished she could take his hand in hers, but she couldn't muster up the courage to do so. This may have made for a bonding between the pair, but once again that untouchable heart of Pimchan's had let her down. As they reached the house, she said goodbye to him at the gate, as she didn't want to see her in-laws. She longed to bend down and give him a goodbye kiss, but once again, it never happened.

Now it was time to find work. Pimchan made her way

back to the sweatshop, as this is what she knew. The same head lady was still there and she recognised Pimchan. She was a good reliable worker so she told her to come back tomorrow and she could start work. Pimchan was happy about this as she needed money. She hoped she could stay at the flat for a while longer as she had to buy a little gas cooker out of her first pay; the rest would have to be sent home to support Mali.

That night she told Pravat she had a job back at the factory, then asked him if she could stay a little longer. "For a little while," he told her. Pimchan could see he was happy, his new girlfriend made him laugh, she even laughed with her, as she was always telling funny stories. She remembered the first night when she lay on Pravat's bed in his dormitory at the leather factory, and what had happened, but then that led to good times under his blanket. She often wondered why he didn't like her any more; she couldn't see in herself how often she crawled into her world of silence. She would find that quiet place to be by herself not wanting to talk, just to shut out the world … but why? Because of her lack of communication no one understood what brought on these moods. Life would have been so much easier for her if she knew of worldly things, like giving birth and being able to express her feelings outwardly. She never expressed any pain, it was always held within, and this is why she couldn't understand why girls cried out while in childbirth. But she could shed tears when needed, the feelings were there, they just couldn't be expressed outwardly. She and Pravat never mentioned the word love. They mustn't have loved each other. Sex was just that, sex, but with this came consequences. She didn't know how to love, to give of herself. Would she ever be able to find love?

At night as she lay on the mattress next to Pravat's bed, she had to listen to the giggles and noises coming from his bed. She would bury her head under her blanket to try to silence her sobbing. She had never looked at another man since being asked to leave. It all became too much for Pimchan, she couldn't take it any longer lying there listening to the fun being had in the bed next to her. Why wasn't it her there, lying with Pravat in their bed?

It was time to take her leave. Now she was back sleeping on the factory floor, sobbing along with many other girls. She missed not seeing Chai, but to him she was still a stranger. She hoped Mali would remember her as her mother next time they met, but this was the sad reality that faced these poor girls.

The sweatshop had changed. She didn't know many of the girls there now, as many were lost to the lads at the leather factory, either as lovers or wives. They still congregated in the alleyway outside the sweatshop hoping to snare a girl, but this time Pimchan was not going to flash one of her beautiful smiles, she was still hurting. Her smiles were her redeeming feature but these would not be seen for a very long time. She now knew what the machine in the bathroom housed: it supplied free condoms. If only she had asked someone, she might not have found herself pregnant in the first place. Perhaps she might have still been with Pravat?

Another year had passed and it was nearing time for Pimchan to take her holidays so she could go home to Mali. But that very day she was told by the factory head that she was needed at home as her daughter was sick. She caught the first possible bus to Sisaket, then another to Kantharalak. When she saw Mali, she was very hot with a high temperature. Pimchan went and fetched a medicine man who confirmed she had pneumonia, so she sat with her and bathed her forehead to keep her temperature down. He prescribed healing herbs for her to take.

It took five months before Mali completely recovered, and Pimchan had spent all this time with her. Now money was becoming a problem once again. Her sister, Lawana, had taken time off work to visit her children who were still with their grandparents. Nothing had changed in their lives. They could not afford to have only one parent working, so the years passed and they still weren't together as a family. During this visit it was a chance for Lawana and Pimchan to catch up. They talked about money and Lawana told her sister that her friend was going down to Phuket to work in a bar as a hostess, as they earned good money. Also, this was the place to meet foreign men, maybe fall in love and be taken to a Western country where life was so much easier. The thought of more money interested Pimchan but the other subject certainly did not! Unfortunately, Lawana was not the right build, nor did she have the looks to be a hostess, but she told her sister,

"When you smile, you are really pretty." That night while lying on her mat, Pimchan could not get this thought out of her head. Was this the turning point for her? If it was better money than the sweatshop, she wouldn't have to listen to the new girls lying under their blankets at night sobbing.

10

WAS THIS A NEW BEGINNING FOR PIMCHAN?

LAWANA'S FRIEND and Pimchan were on their way to Phuket to try their luck as bar hostesses. There were many types of bars and entertainment, each having different expectations from the girls. Pimchan was happy when she saw the sign 'No touching policy' in one of the beachfront bars. Depending on what you offered was what you were paid. Lawana's friend wanted to earn big money so she went to the other end of the scale to what Pimchan was prepared to earn.

The hostesses' primary job was to offer polite conversation and encourage the patrons to drink. They were given instructions to find out about the surrounding attractions and each was given lessons on body massage. But it was not uncommon for Asian girls to have had experience in this field, as it was encouraged at home on elderly family members. Most of the males that holidayed in Phuket did not come for the scenery, they came for the girls. The one good point Pimchan had over most of the other girls was she could speak a little English. Very basic, in fact, but she knew enough words to hold a polite conversation, and this she was thankful for. Her self-teaching had paid off!

The girls that spoke very little English had to flirt more to attract the patrons. Most bars worked on a commission system, paying the hostesses a percentage of their bar sales. If the patron shouted the hostess a drink it would be charged at inflated bar prices, when in fact it was non-alcoholic, to ensure the girls didn't get inebriated. With this came the rights for the patron to purchase the hostess's attention for a set period of time.

Pimchan didn't find it easy at the start, as her quiet nature kept her lurking in the back of the bar, but sometimes this had its advantages. If a patron was quiet within themselves, they sought the least outgoing girl. Most of the younger girls were provocative and outgoing, they had to be to draw the patrons in, this was their living. After six months working as a hostess Pimchan was earning good money, but she was still the elusive background girl. It was her English that helped her immensely, as sometimes this is what a patron wanted, to hold a conversation in English.

One day a youngish foreign male came to the bar for a drink. This was not unusual; he was quite tall, had dark hair, was good-looking and well dressed. He appeared to be on his own and was a Westerner. The hostesses all vied for his attention. He didn't query the exorbitant bar prices and was quite happy to shout a hostess a drink. He seemed very pleasant and in need of company. He sat and had several drinks, then off he went. This stranger was the topic of conversation among the hostesses. Who was he? But because they couldn't speak English, no one found out much about him. They hoped they would see him again tomorrow.

Each day for a week he came to the bar and had his couple of bourbons and Coke and shouted for a hostess. One day he came back from the markets with a bowl of fruit for the girls and left it on the bar. This was a surprise, as this didn't happen very often, in fact it never happened. Who was this kind man? Why did he come each day? Unbeknown to anyone he kept coming to the bar just to see the girl lurking in the background. A couple of times when he looked her way, she flashed him a smile and it was that smile that drew him back. The girls at the front bar were taken by this foreigner, not for a minute thinking it was Pimchan who was the drawcard. She was never out the front, but if someone requested her then she had to become their hostess.

The young man asked the manager if he could buy her a drink so he went and fetched her. Out she came and smiled at him and sat down but did not say a word. He offered to buy her a drink and she accepted, as was expected of her. Now she was his hostess for a set time. "What is your name?" he asked. "I am Pimchan." "Pleased to meet you, Pimchan. I am James, I am holidaying from New Zealand. Where do you come from?" he asked her. "I am from Kantharalak," she answered. "Where is that?" She explained it was a little Thai village near the Laos-Cambodian border. Then all went silent. James could see she wasn't giving much away so he didn't press for any more information. He was pleased to think he could converse with her in English. They sat and finished their drinks in silence. James then decided to leave as he felt she had finished with him. As he left, Pimchan smiled at him and said, "Thank you, James." When James was out of earshot, she was reprimanded by the bar manager for not talking to him and keeping him there longer, as he might have bought more drinks. "That's what you are here for, to keep the customers drinking," he spoke with her angrily. He was thinking of his livelihood; he could have got the profits from another couple of drinks.

The next day James decided to stay away from the bar, so he walked to the markets. He was blown away by the merchandise that was on sale. He saw many baskets of beautiful tropical fruit and thought back to the bar girls. They were really happy with the last basket he dropped off, so he purchased another one. He would deliver it on his way back to the hotel. As he passed the bar he stopped and the girls came running out. He gave them the fruit to share, then carried on. They were disappointed he didn't stay for a drink and so was the manager, as it was money he was missing out on. Was he drinking at another bar? "Next time this stranger comes back, I expect you all to make a fuss of him," he told the girls, while thinking of his own pocket.

The first week of James's holiday was over, and he still had another two weeks to go. He had decided on the spur of the moment to fly to Phuket. Was it because he had heard about the lovely girls? No, it was because he had broken up with his Japanese wife of eight years. She wanted the world and he couldn't give it to her. She was a Japanese interpreter and used to a life of travel and excitement. She was not interested in settling down and having a family, she was a career lady going places. James could not afford her the life she so desired, so they separated. He had sold his house and given her half the money, hence why he was holidaying. He had been lonely since he arrived, which was why he drank at the bar so he had company, but he also liked to have a drink.

Today he would go back and see if he could see Pimchan. Her smile had won him over, but she was very elusive, not at all a talkative soul. Perhaps that would change with time? At least she understood a little English, this he was happy for. When he arrived at the bar he was treated like a long-lost friend. The bar owner even shouted him his first drink, as he knew several paid ones would follow. These people were not silly, they were sharp and could see potential punters. He asked James, "You want to pay for Pimchan for a day? You give me twenty dollars?" James was taken by surprise as he had seen the 'No touching bar' sign on the wall, so didn't think for a minute he could take her away for the day. "Yes, but only if Pimchan would like to come with me?" James asked. She came out from behind the bar and sat next to him. He asked to buy her a drink so they sat until they finished, then they left together. "Where would you like to go?" he asked her. "Can we go to the beach?" so off they walked in that direction.

Unless James talked, Pimchan remained silent, but she would cast glances his way and flash her beautiful smile. They lay on the warm sand together with the sun beating upon them. After a while she sat up and leaned over and started massaging his shoulders. James enjoyed this immensely, then her hands moved down his back. He could feel her palms pushing hard on his pressure points. He relaxed and asked her for more as this felt so good. When her hands tired, she lay down next to James and he reached out and took hold of her hand. This was the way they stayed for the next few hours with neither speaking a word.

The afternoon was nearly over so James asked Pimchan if he could take her for dinner. She chose a Thai restaurant so they sat together and she explained the menu to him, then they ordered. "Tell me a little about yourself, Pimchan." "I have been married and have two children, a boy and a girl," she told him. "Where are they now?" James asked. She explained in pidgin English that they were with different grandparents. "Why don't they live together as brother and sister?" James was curious to know. "My husband only wanted the son; he didn't want me or the girl so he asked us to leave." James was stunned by this explanation … why? The meal arrived so they stopped talking and began eating. Again, silence befell this couple. After they had eaten, James took her hand and they walked back to the bar. Pimchan thanked him and disappeared behind the bar.

James ordered a drink. "You happy with her?" asked the owner. "Yes, we had a nice day, but she is a silent girl, doesn't say much," James told him. "She very shy, doesn't like spending a day with a man, that is why she work here 'No touching bar'," and he pointed to the sign above the bar. This intrigued James; why did she agree to come with him for the day? he had to ask. "I think she like you, all the girls like you, but Pimchan more," he answered. This hit a chord with James as he felt drawn to her, but she was really hard going. "Pimchan very poor, very poor and very shy and sad. She smiles for you, you lucky," he told James. As James left the bar and walked back to his hotel, he thought long and hard about Pimchan. He really felt deep down in his heart for her, what a sad life for a young mother, having to live without her children, especially being told to leave with one child and splitting the family, but he knew little of the Thai culture.

The next day Pimchan looked out for James but he did not come. She was sad, she wanted him to come back. This was the first time she had felt this way about someone. He did not want anything from her when he had her for the day, he was nice to her and bought her dinner. He didn't try to touch her, perhaps he didn't like her, she had mixed feelings now. She would just have to wait until tomorrow. But tomorrow brought no joy; he did not come back. She was sad, as was everyone else at the bar, including the manager.

Unbeknown to all, James was not well and had spent the next two days in bed, all the time thinking about Pimchan. Why did she not talk? He had never met anyone like her before. Would she be a worry? he wondered. Perhaps if she was happy, she might be different and open up a little more. Why was he thinking like this? He had just met her and knew very little about her. He waited another day until he went back to the bar, as he didn't want the girls to catch his bug. This meant he had been missing for three days. Pimchan wondered where he was, perhaps he had moved on. She didn't think she would ever see him again. But the next day there he was, making his way to the bar, and this made her very happy. She had not felt this happiness before, not even with Pravat. Was she finding love in her heart? Perhaps it shouldn't be, she told herself, as he was a Westerner and she was Asian. When his holiday was over, he would go back to his home country and she would never see him again. Pimchan would have to let go of these feelings; she felt they were going to lead to heartbreak.

As he came to the bar, he saw Pimchan looking at him. She flashed him one of those beautiful smiles that made him feel that she liked him. He wasn't ready to drink alcohol so he ordered a soft drink for himself and one for Pimchan and asked for her to be his hostess. They sat together. "Why you not come for three days?" she asked. "I have been in bed for two days; I had a bug." "I'm sorry," she answered and looked at the ground. He asked her to look at him. "Don't be sorry. I missed you, Pimchan." This brought a little smile from her but she wasn't giving too much away, she had been hurt before. They continued to sit in silence until James told her he was going to have something to eat. "You come back?" she asked. He decided to leave this question open to see what she said next. "I'm not sure what I will do." "I like it if you come back to see me," she told him. This was what James wanted to hear, some recognition of how she felt towards him. Now he knew perhaps she did feel a little something for him. "I will see you later," he said as he left.

After he had eaten, he decided he might go to a night-club, as he was still recovering from his bug and didn't feel like drinking. He wanted to have a nosy to see what they entailed. As he made his way along the streets there were young girls, in fact many were just kids, all trying to snare foreigners. They were touching them trying to find one that would pay to spend a night with them. James was horrified as he was not into this, they were just kids selling their bodies for sex with strange men. They couldn't speak English so how did they know where they were going to be taken or what was going to happen to them? Some men were ruthless! Just being among these young girls was shock enough for James. He turned around and made his way back to the bar.

At least the hostess girls were not young girls, they were old enough to know what life was about. To most of the young street girls, it was the hope of finding a foreigner who would take them back to their country with the promise of a better life. For the rural poor girls, the only prospect of work was in a factory or as a bar hostess and, worse still, that of prostitution. The prospect of a decent job was bleak indeed. Because their families couldn't afford to keep them, they had to find work of some kind. It was hard to understand other cultures, especially when coming from a Western background. James hoped to learn more through Pimchan, as she had an understanding of English, although quite limited, but he was a patient young man. Pimchan eagerly waited for James to return. She knew if she wanted to become friends with him, she would have to talk more, otherwise he might choose someone else. He still had another ten days left in Phuket.

11

A TRIAL TOGETHER

OVER THE NEXT eight days James actually learnt about Pimchan's life, as she had opened up. He now decided he didn't want to go back to New Zealand so he applied for an extension to his visa. To do this he had to leave Thailand and cross a border to get his passport stamped from another country, just to show he had left the country. The closest border to Phuket was Myanmar. He paid the bar owner to have Pimchan for another day so they both caught a bus to Myanmar. James got his passport stamped. He didn't have to stay — as long as he had proof that he had left Thailand, he could come straight back over the border. He was happy to have Pimchan with him, as she knew the language; she was an asset when it came to dealing with border matters.

A close relationship was forming between them. James decided to bring the rest of his money over from New Zealand and hire a nice apartment, then he asked Pimchan to come and share it with him. She still wanted to do her hostess job, as she had to send money home to her parents for Mali. James agreed, as it was a 'No touching bar' so no men could grope her. He was not allowed to work in Thailand as he was on a visitor's permit, so he made the most of the sun, surf and sea. After four months living the good life and several more trips across the border to get his passport stamped, James's money tree had lost most of its leaves, so he now had to work out a budget. Pimchan decided to leave her job as a bar hostess, as she wanted to take James home to meet her parents and Mali and let him experience what poverty was really like. James had a lot of adjusting to do while living with Pimchan, as she was certainly different. It was her silent periods that bothered him, but he felt the more time they spent together this would change, as at this moment they were still virtual strangers trying to sort their lives out together. He did enjoy her massage sessions; there must also have been other benefits!

On their arrival at Kantharalak, James was appalled by the living conditions of Pimchan's family and indeed a lot of the village people. Her home, or rather shelter, was on a block of land forty by forty metres square, shared with hens, two pigs and a buffalo. He could not believe the poverty that surrounded these people. Pimchan's parents could not speak English so James could only talk to them through her. He met Mali. She was a tiny dot for a three-year-old, but a happy soul, and James took an instant liking to her. Mali took a little while to come around, as she hadn't seen her mother for over a year so she was like a stranger to her. Pimchan felt sad as this reminded her of Chai, the same scenario!

When it came to meal time James was happy he had brought supplies with him, as Pimchan had warned him what would be served for meals. Just to see the insects being fried over the fire in a wok-type pan was enough, but the salad and rice looked okay, he was sure he could eat this. As soon as darkness set in, they all spread their mats on the floor and slept together in one room. James was learning very quickly what life was like in a rural poor area. It was hot and sticky in the shelter, there were no fans or air-conditioning. It was just as it was, the naked truth, no frills!

After a couple of days of settling in, Pimchan took James to the temple. He was intrigued with the monks when they came around on their alms walk, ringing their bells to let the village folk know they were coming with their offering bowls to collect food. He was keen to learn about their lives and their beliefs; it was of great interest to him as he was right into world affairs. The monks were very friendly and spoke to him about their lives, humble as they were, but their sole purpose was to serve their gods. They spent a lot of time chanting and in prayer, but also were teachers to the young novice monks from the poor areas, who couldn't afford to pay for schooling.

James noticed a couple of moped motorcycles around the area. It was not unusual to see up to four people at any one time on these cycles. One day he noticed a man on one of these motorcycles carrying a bag over his shoulders and whatever he had in the bag was moving. He asked Pimchan what he was doing. "He is buying dogs from the people." "What on earth for?" asked James. "They are used as meat for the restaurants." James was mortified, as all the dogs he had seen were skinny half-fed animals, probably riddled with fleas and diseased. But this was life as such, and he was learning fast.

James had made a friend in Mali, who followed him everywhere, as did Lawana's boys, Art and Bart. He would take them all up to the little store and buy them sweets. He made them a trolley out of rubbish materials he found lying around, and there was plenty, and they loved it. They all took turns at pulling the little ones around, and it became the property of all the village children. Nothing was owned outright, everything was jointly owned by everyone.

James noticed a couple of Pimchan's uncles were partial to having a drink, but being poor they couldn't afford to buy bottles of alcohol. When they saw James with a bottle of bourbon, they all came over and stayed until it was finished. He had to be mindful though, as her father had become addicted very easily. In the end he learnt to do what all poor people do — go to the store and buy a nip of whatever and drink it over the counter. It was like cigarettes; everyone would borrow them off James when they saw him with a packet. After a while he became wise and like everyone else, he would buy one at a time over the counter at the store, then no one could borrow.

He laughed when he first saw this happening, but it

didn't take long for him to realise that these people all lived off each other and shared what they had; it was the only way they could survive. Pimchan's mother was not seen very often as she was always away gathering food. James felt sorry for her as she didn't wear footwear and her feet were large and spread out. He noticed her toes were like claws, and this fascinated him. She looked older than what she was and didn't seem to care about her appearance … but really, who would have noticed? James began to understand why Pimchan was different. Her life was one born out of poverty, with very little verbal conversation or outward affection. If she had not left this village, her life may not have been any different to that of her mother's. Looking in from the outside, life was tough for these people but it was a life of acceptance and survival … they knew no other!

Lawana and her husband tried to get to see their children as often as they could. Her husband loved his children but poverty did not allow them to live together as a normal family. Would this ever be able to happen? It wasn't looking promising any time soon. But this was accepted as normal. Most families were faced with the same problem, and grandparents became the guardians of their grandchildren while the parents worked in the city to send money home. It was just how life was. The elderly didn't receive any money from the government so relied on their children to keep them. It was a communal way of life, and the children entertained themselves for the majority of the time.

CAMBODIA — A LITTLE HISTORY

TODAY PIMCHAN and James were crossing over the border into Cambodia. James had to get his passport stamped to show he had left the country, as his time was due to expire again. He was very vigilant in keeping his records straight for fear of being evicted from Thailand. This would make it impossible for him to re-enter, so he did everything that was expected of him as a visitor. This was the closest border to where Pimchan's parents lived.

As they neared the Cambodian border, the level of poverty was much harsher than what they experienced in their own little village, almost to the point of James wanting to turn back. The stark realisation of just how poverty stricken these border villages were brought James to tears. This was the result of many Laos citizens leaving their country during Pol Pot's brutal reign and never being allowed to return. They were outcasts.

They had decided to stay in Cambodia for a night so

they could visit the temple of Angkor Wat, the largest religious monument in the world. Thank goodness for Pimchan's knowledge on how to travel, otherwise James would have been tested to the limit. There were two options — by bus or by train. Pimchan knew to take a more expensive bus, then they were guaranteed of reaching their destination. The cheaper buses were not properly maintained so it was a lucky-dip with them, nothing could be assured! It was roughly a four-and-a-half-hour trip from Sisaket to Angkor Wat, but of course this depended on the stamping of James's passport at the border and if any questions were put to him by the border patrol. Again, James was thankful he was travelling with Pimchan as she spoke their language and it made it so much easier to be travelling with a Thai citizen. The border guards were intimidating and James felt a little uncomfortable. This was when Pimchan came to the fore. She answered the questions and his passport was stamped. This was a new side to Pimchan, one James had never seen before. Were there still things he didn't know about her? They caught another bus to the village of Siem Reap where they found a little boarding house for the night. It was cheap but comfortable. Tomorrow they would visit the temple.

The temple of Angkor Wat ('city of temples') is set in the Cambodian jungle on 402 acres of land that has been terraced and raised higher than the city. It was originally constructed as a Hindu temple dedicated to the god Vishnu for the Khmer empire, then gradually transforming into a Buddhist temple in the early twelfth century. The splendid artistic legacy of Angkor Wat and other Khmer monuments in the Angkor region led directly to France adopting Cambodia as a protectorate in 1863. It invaded Siam (Thailand) to take control of the ruins. This quickly led to Cambodia reclaiming land in the northwestern corner of the country that had been taken under Siamese (Thai) control since 1351. Cambodia gained independence from France in 1953 and has controlled Angkor Wat since. From the fifteenth to the eighteenth centuries, Theravada Buddhist monks cared for Angkor Wat and it is thanks to them that the temple remains mostly intact. No one lives at the temple but it has become one of the most important pilgrimage sites in South-East Asia. Buddhist monks are daily visitors to Angkor Wat.

The Khmer Rouge originated in the 1960s as the armed wing of the Communist Party of Kampuchea (Cambodia); often they were just teenagers. It gradually increased its control in the countryside and then Khmer Rouge forces finally took over the capital, Phnom Penh, and the nation as a whole in 1975. Khmer Rouge's brutal regime was in power from 1975 to 1979 under the Marxist leader Pol Pot. During his time in the remote northeast, he had been influenced by the surrounding hill tribes, who were self-sufficient in their communal living. They had no use for money and were 'untainted' by Buddhism. Pol Pot tried to take Cambodia back to the Middle Ages, forcing millions of people from the cities to work on communal farms in the countryside. He was isolating his people from the rest of the world, emptying cities, abolishing money, private property and religion, setting up rural collectives. But this dramatic attempt at social engineering came at a terrible cost. Whole families died from execution, starvation, disease and overwork. Anyone thought to be intelligent, along with hundreds of thousands of educated middle class, was tortured and executed in special centres.

The Khmer Rouge government was finally overthrown in 1979 by invading Vietnamese troops after a series of border confrontations. They retreated back to the jungle, but in years to come they still caused small periods of unrest.

As James and Pimchan approached the temple grounds they were in disbelief. Such magnificent ruins and so old. How did they construct these marvels? James had never seen the likes, he was stunned. Just looking at this religious site brought a peace of mind, a feeling of solitude and rest. The history of this area was breathtaking. To think this crumbling temple was built in the twelfth century and had seen so many battles fought around and over the ownership of it. James touch the walls to get a closer feeling to this holy place and thought, if only they could talk, what stories could they tell? There were monks in their orange robes paying homage to this special place of prayer. Some were kneeling, others sitting in the lotus position. It was a meeting place, and to many they had come to the end of their pilgrimage.

Pimchan elected to wander off on her own, to retreat into her own little world. She sat on a step then went into the lotus position and started a meditation. She didn't want to listen to James rambling on; he was so excited he couldn't keep it to himself, he just wanted to express and share how he felt about the whole experience. Hence the difference in cultures. Was this telling him something, something he didn't pick up on? It was then he spotted a monk walking towards him so he stopped him to have a chat. He told James he had reached the end of his pilgrimage. He had been here many times before and would continue to come many times into the future, to pay his thanks and respect to the Theravada monks who protected this precious religious temple during times of hardship. James felt at home talking to the monks, as he had talked to them at the temple in Pimchan's village. He did not feel at all intimidated by them. He felt they were special people who were not afraid to share their thoughts with those who asked questions of them.

As much as he wanted to stay and take in more of this fantastic atmosphere, it was time to think about making a move as they had to cross the border back into Thailand. James watched Pimchan, who was in deep meditation, and he felt sad they had to leave Angkor Wat. He tapped her on the shoulder bringing her out of her personal silence. She stretched and stood up, so James took her hand and they stood together, each thinking in their own minds the peace and calm they had felt in this place of ancient worship. It truly deserved to be included as one of the seven wonders of the world. They vowed to come back; this would not be their last visit.

The bus ride home was time for reflection on what was

a short visit to Cambodia. Apart from the hostile look on the faces of the border patrol guards and the harsh poverty of the families living near the border, Cambodia was a delight to visit with its incredible history and temples. Now it was back to a not-so-harsh life of poverty in Kantharalak with Pimchan's family, when compared to what they had seen earlier that day.

13

SAD GOODBYES

JAMES'S MONEY was running out. The money from the sale of his house in New Zealand was all but gone. He had no regrets as he had been able to share some of it with Pimchan, turning her life around, giving her a little taste of what life could be like. He told her all about New Zealand and what money she could earn if she came out and worked, but above all, the standard of living was so different to what she was used to. The only downside was leaving her children. But because she had virtually been separated from them most of their young lives and only saw them once a year, it probably didn't matter where she lived, as long as she could fly back and see them every so often. The separate grandparents who lived in different parts of Thailand were the children's guardians, they had been there for them all their lives. The siblings had not seen each other since Pimchan was told to leave with Mali.

Pravat was starting a new family with his young lover,

so now Chai lived full time with his grandparents. They lived east of Bangkok and Mali lived way to the west, many miles apart. James thought this was sad that they never knew each other, but Pravat would not let Chai come to see his mother. Hopefully that would change one day! Mali was still too young to understand she had a brother. She had all the village kids to play with, so this was not a big deal at the moment.

The time had come for James to leave Pimchan, as he had to travel back to New Zealand and earn money. They had talked things over: when he had saved enough, he would apply for a visitor's visa so Pimchan could come to New Zealand; he would have to be her sponsor. He knew he would miss her. She was one silent mysterious girl, not plain sailing to deal with, but was that the attraction? Did he think he could change her once away from her sad environment? Time would tell. They wanted to spend their last night together on their own, in privacy, to say their final farewells, so James booked a hotel room at Sisaket away from family members. This must be where Pimchan was at her best, in the bedroom where no words had to be spoken!

The next morning James caught the bus to Bangkok and Pimchan headed back to her family and her daughter. She had to give some thought as to what she was going to do for work, as the family needed money, she had to support them and Mali. Lawana's three children were still living with the grandparents, but sometimes she didn't send money home and this caused great problems. Pimchan would wait a few days as James had left a little money for her to get back to Phuket if she wanted to do more hostess work but only on the condition it was at the same 'No touching bar'. This was his request. He would spend the night in Bangkok then catch his flight home. He was looking forward to some cooler weather as autumn was just starting. It would be a shock to James's system when he began work, as he had been a man of leisure for the past six months.

He was not a man of extravagant needs; as long as he could survive, have a few drinks, his vision of the future was put on hold, he lived for today. He had a brilliant career as a resort manager with a Japanese company in Australia but that all disappcarcd when he chose the wrong path. He had a turbulent few years, that of his own doing, and lost the ambitious will that he once had. The future was just that, the future. Perhaps there wasn't going to be a future so he lived for today. The wonderful quality he had was a kind heart — he would give his last cent to someone if they needed it more than him. He would never hurt a fly. He knew what it was like to suffer, as he had reached rock bottom but had managed to claw himself back. Was this the attraction to Pimchan? Did he feel they had something in common? Is this why a friendship had developed between them in the first place? The shy girl in the bar, not the prettiest but the one with the beautiful smile. Were their stars aligned?

With the harsh winter over and the pruning finished, James had money in the bank so he went to apply for a tourist visa for Pimchan. She had to fill out papers via the

Thai authorities and he was listed as her sponsor. Sadly, New Zealand immigration turned her down due to lack of money on her behalf. As she wasn't able to work here on a tourist visa, she had no money to keep herself. It took another year before Pimchan finally arrived in New Zealand. She had been granted a three-month tourist visa. She arrived in the spring; the warmer weather was thankfully arriving as she was used to forty-degree temperatures. Her English had not improved, it had come to a standstill, so James would have to try to persuade her to take English lessons. These were available at the local Reap office. He could understand her most of the time, but to a stranger she was not easy to understand. Her shyness didn't help, especially in a strange country, and this did little to boost her confidence.

James took her places at weekends when he wasn't working, to show her the area. One of the first trips was to an Asian supermarket in the city so she could buy Thai ingredients, especially rice. James cooked his own meals, as Pimchan was not used to cooking Western food. There was one meat she could not bring herself to eat and that was lamb, which she called ghat. One found it hard to believe that she could eat any insect, but not lamb? How strange!

Nearing the end of her three months they applied for a working holiday permit, so her visitor's visa was extended for another three months. Because there was a shortage of fruit pickers in the area, she was able to get work through an organisation that brought in foreign workers. Her wage was paid by the orchardist to the organisation, which took out ten per cent then deposited the balance into her personal bank account. Pimchan was happy to be able to work, as she could then send money back to Thailand to her family. She was totally amazed at how much she could earn compared to what she was paid in Thailand, but then, living was more expensive here. She was a good worker and would work as many hours as was asked of her. She and James worked the fruit season together and saved money, as they wanted to go back to Thailand to see the children.

After the fruit season had finished, James flew to Wellington with Pimchan to apply for residency. This took ages to process and hundreds of dollars later, the forms arrived for her to fill out. As long as her residency was being processed, she was allowed to stay in New Zealand. Once this was signed, sealed and delivered, Pimchan was able to live and work here permanently. James was still having difficulty with her silent periods; sometimes she wouldn't speak for several days, and this he found nerve-racking, as he liked to talk. He couldn't fully understand why this was still happening as she was away from the poverty in Thailand. Was this a cultural difference? Would she change?

14

A VISIT HOME TO THAILAND

JAMES AND PIMCHAN were on their way back to Thailand to see Mali. James suggested that Pimchan ring Chai's grandparents to see if they could pick him up and take him on holiday with Mali, as a family. The children had not seen each other since Pravat asked her to leave the flat with her daughter. Mali was due to start school and Chai was seven years old. They caught the bus from Bangkok to Sisaket, where they bought a bike for Mali with money from James's parents. Then they travelled on to Kanthar-alak. Once again Pimchan was a stranger to her daughter, although she was now old enough to know of her mother, but it would take a few days for her to come around. The bike was well received as it was the newest toy in the village, thus, of course, everyone wanted to ride it. Mali didn't mind sharing it during the day but at night it had to be hidden so no one could touch it. Although the youngest grandchild, she was the one in charge, she was the bossy boots. Lawana's three children were still living with the grandparents as she and her husband were still working in the city and sending money home. At this stage there was no sign of them ever being able to live together as a family.

After a few days with Pimchan's parents, James wanted to move on. The heat was unbearable, there was nothing to combat it, they just lived with it. Arrangements had been made to pick up Chai at his grandparents' house, so there was a full day's travel to reach him. They travelled by bus to where Chai lived. Pimchan cried when she saw him, as he had grown so much. He was quite shy and when he met his sister, they just stared at each other. How was this going to pan out? They booked into a hotel for a night before they travelled to Phuket so the siblings could get to know each other. They were virtual strangers although they were brother and sister. Chai was standoffish with Mali, and she showed her dominance right from the start. Chai was not used to having a younger person around, as he was quite independent. Was this the start of sibling rivalry?

The next morning, they left to travel to Phuket as neither child had seen the sea. James had booked accommodation in a seaside resort for a week. When they arrived, they settled into their unit then decided to go for a walk along the beach. The kids were excited as this was all new to them. All along the beach there were clothing stalls, mostly catering for the female species. Mali saw a sun dress she wanted. "Can I have this dress? I like it," she said. Pimchan gave her the money to buy it. "That's not fair. What can I buy?" asked Chai. All there was was clothes for girls so he decided he wanted a dress also. This brought laughter from the adults, who told Chai he was not allowed a dress. The sibling rivalry had started!

It took several days before brother and sister formed any sort of friendship. James took Chai away for a day to a fishing village where they paid to hire fishing gear and to catch fish. There were hundreds of people with the same idea, so they were allocated a spot by the pond to fish. It was difficult for James as Chai didn't speak English. After about an hour with neither catching anything, Chai went off in a huff and sat on a seat under a tree. This left James fishing on his own. He knew it would be difficult for him at times, but he was a patient being and didn't let any of this upset him. God knows he struggled with Pimchan at times, this couldn't be any worse. Eventually Chai made his way back and picked up his rod. Several people caught fish but not James or Chai. Never mind, James felt they needed bonding time away from the girls. The language barrier was a huge bugbear, but James managed to cope.

They took the children to the zoo and had lovely photos taken of them as a family with the animals. Pimchan and Mali wanted to go to the markets so they all went and James shouted the kids things they wanted to buy, as he wanted this to be a memorable holiday. They loved the sea and played in the sand, while Pimchan massaged James's shoulders and back, bringing back memories of their first meetings. Because the kids lived inland, this was their first time at the beach. Pimchan's mother was sixty and had never been to the seaside, let alone ever seen the sea; her life never afforded her such luxuries. Perhaps this word was not in her vocabulary. As the holiday was nearing an end the children's differences had been put aside and a family bond was slowly forming. Pimchan's silent periods were still persistent and James noticed she had trouble expressing feelings, even towards her children. Was this because she felt they were strangers or was it because of her background?

It was time to say their goodbyes as they delivered Chai home to his grandparents. He thanked them for taking him on holiday and shook James's hand. Pimchan gave him a cuddle of sorts. It was an unemotional parting as their lives were not going to be any different; it would be back to the same old, same old. When would he see his mother again? She was still this stranger who popped in and out of his life, disappearing for long periods of time. But by the grace of God, brother and sister had met and now they were old enough to remember each other. Hopefully this was the beginning of a friendship that would remain intact. They took Mali back to her grandparents and stayed for a night before heading back to Bangkok. As soon as Mali arrived home, she was away looking for the village kids, her holiday probably forgotten already, but she was still young. James was the one who felt happy about the holiday, as he had reunited a brother and sister.

James and Pimchan had a few days to themselves in Bangkok before they flew back to New Zealand. They visited temples and shrines thus stirring up feelings between them both. It was here they made the biggest decision of their lives. Outside the Royal Palace, James asked Pimchan to marry him. It was a spur-of-the-moment proposal. Pimchan agreed to wed James, so he dashed away and bought a white shirt for himself and a lovely bunch of flowers for his bride. They took their vows in front of a huge portrait of the Thai king, as the Thai people loved him dearly, he was their father. Thousands of Thai couples married in this very place, as it was sacred, and to have their beloved king share their wedding photo was indeed an honour. Now that they were husband and wife, would life become easier for them both? Would there be changes in Pimchan's moods?

15

LIFE MOVES FORWARD

ANOTHER FIVE YEARS had passed and the marriage had struck many turbulent patches, but they somehow managed to salvage it, hopefully with better times ahead. James and Pimchan had a variety of jobs — they worked in orchards and then in vineyards for two seasons until they moved to a new venture that was just starting. They applied for a job as a married couple on a sheep-milking farm and were promised a specified number of hours, but this didn't eventuate, so after six months they left for a married couple's job on a dairy farm. If the hours weren't enough on the last farm, they were certainly made up for on the dairy farm.

James started work at 4 am. He had to bring the cows from the paddock to the milking shed, where Pimchan started milking at 5 am. At nine o'clock they had an hour for breakfast then went back out to work until lunch time at 1 pm. Pimchan didn't have to start back until three o'clock to do the next milking. James worked through to between 6 pm and 7.30 pm. The saving grace was their farm house, which was a lovely three-bedroom brick and roughcast home with beautiful gardens. As there were three homes on the property, a gardener came in and mowed the lawns and looked after the gardens, simply because the farm workers had very little spare time. They were worked to the bone, as was well known in the dairy industry. There were some ruthless employers out there. Pimchan didn't mind the long hours as it was more money for her, and she could send a little extra home. Now that her family knew she was making good money, they played on this and their demands grew greater. Her brother's marriage had ended and even he was on the phone looking for money. This was Chetak who had his parents sell their property for his wedding dowry. Pimchan didn't call her family for several weeks sometimes, as sadly, it was always a plea for more money.

When their holidays were due after a year working on the dairy farm, they flew back to Thailand to see the children. Mali was now ten and Chai nearly thirteen. Again, James wanted them to go on holiday as a family as the children had not seen each other since their last holiday five years ago. This time it would be a little easier because Chai and Mali knew each other, they wouldn't be total strangers, but of course they had both grown up. This time they holidayed on the coast at a new place called Prachuap, which was a popular holiday resort. It was bonding time for Chai and Mali. James was easy to get on with. He was a very even-tempered guy, he had to be, sometimes having to stand in for Pimchan when her silent periods emerged. Now that the children were older, their wants had changed, and more time was spent hanging out at the shopping malls looking to see what they could con out of their mother and James. This was their big chance to spend. Phones and computers had taken over from ordinary toys. Chai and Mali became the proud owners of a modern phone each, so now they could keep in touch with each other and Pimchan could call them from New Zealand. There was a hint of a computer, but that was going to have to wait.

All too soon, the holiday was nearly over. They had taken Chai back to his grandparents and were now back in Kantharalak with Pimchan's parents. One night her father and uncles managed to acquire some alcohol and started a drinking session along with James. As they became more intoxicated, they started picking on James and a fun fight developed into a full-blown fist fight. Pimchan was angry with James so he left the village and staggered along the road until he ended up collapsing on the temple steps. When he woke in the morning, he found himself on a mattress inside the temple. An old monk found him and brought him inside where he would be safe. James was very remorseful, and grateful to the monks for their kindness.

He liked visiting the temple as he had good talks with

the monks, finding them really interesting. They were in fact ordinary young men who held a greater appreciation of their religious beliefs, living a life of sacrifices devoid of everyday comforts, so they could serve and be closer to their gods. Now it was time to say goodbye to Mali as their two-week holiday was over.

BACK ON THE FARM

THEY WERE BACK on the farm where long hours of work awaited them. James liked working with the cows and called them his 'old girls'. At 4 am he would make his way down the paddock on his four-wheeler to wake the cows and bring them up to the milking shed. They would all be lying on the cold grass. He would go up to one and tap her on her rump and she would get up, then others would follow until they were all standing, then the long walk to relief would begin. James felt quite sorry for them lying on the cold ground surrounded by steam coming from their nostrils as they breathed in the cold morning air. They trudged along the gravel lane towards the milking shed. They were in no hurry, they had just woken, their udders were full of milk, but soon there would be some relief. Pimchan began at 5 am, so she was in the shed getting all the computerised equipment ready for her milkers. James would drive the cows onto a platform that revolved to get them into position. In front of them would be troughs filled with palm kernel so they were happy to eat as their milk was being taken from them. The kernel was a welcome change from the green grass, it felt warmer in their bellies. Once milked they were taken to a new paddock where fresh pastures awaited them.

James was out testing the pastures and shifting fences while the milking was in full swing. Many hours were spent shifting electric break fences to give the grass a chance to rejuvenate in the paddocks they had just come from. It was all very technical! Then again at 2 pm he was bringing in the cows for their second milking, which started at 3 pm. It was a vicious cycle for the poor old cows but then again, it would have been a relief to be rid of the milk that was filling their udders. The most hated job on the farm for James was calving time. The day after the calves were born, they were taken away from their mothers and put in a separate paddock until the stock trucks came to take them away. This was where it was good to be born a female as they were kept as milkers, although their lives never amounted to much other than to become a 'cash cow'. The mothers knew something was wrong and they would all line up at the fence and cry out to their babies. James found this heartbreaking. But this was part and parcel of farming!

Several months later, Pimchan had a phone call from Chai to say he had left school and was looking for a job, which was not easy to find in Thailand. His aunty Lawana was trying to get him a job on a construction site where she was now working. He wanted to know if he could get work in New Zealand. Mali was now thirteen, nearly fourteen, and had fallen out with her grandfather because he was putting restrictions on her, stopping her going out at night, so she was also enquiring about coming to live with Pimchan and James.

Thus began the complicated task of trying to bring the siblings to New Zealand to live. There was so much red tape. First of all, they had to pass medical examinations, get Thai passports and New Zealand visas to come here, all costing a lot of money. Their medical examinations had to be undertaken in Thailand under a New Zealand immigration medically approved government associated hospital. If they had any medical problems they would not have been accepted into New Zealand. Because Pimchan had included her children's names on her original visa when she applied for New Zealand residency, it meant the children's names had been on the file for a number of years, thus making it a quicker process. Neither child spoke English, they had not lived together as brother and sister, nor had they ever lived with their mother. This was of great concern to James. How would Pimchan manage the children in her silent periods? She had never been a full-time mother to them. Could she cope?

When it came to filling out the paperwork, she would not let James help. This was her stubbornness. She thought she could manage, although her English was minimal. She found this to be costly, as the paperwork was not filled out correctly. By the time it came back to New Zealand time had lapsed on the children's medicals, so they had to start from scratch and pay again for what had already been done. This was all costing thousands of dollars, with the Thai authorities charging excessively for their part. On top of this Pimchan had to fly to Wellington twice to meet with immigration. James was looking forward to the children coming out as he wanted them to have a better life, and it might make things a little more interesting between himself and Pimchan if there was a family situation. He loved children but never had any of his own. They discussed what they wanted to happen, that there would be rules for the children to abide by.

One year on, all the paperwork was completed so now the children had New Zealand residency, so it was time to fly them out. James and Pimchan pooled their money for the airfares to fly Pimchan back to Thailand and bring Chai and Mali back. James could not go, due to what it had cost them thus far. He had spoken to Pimchan about the difficulties everyone would face, especially with schooling and their lack of understanding the English language, but he didn't think she fully understood how hard it would be for them all. She would just switch off and silence would reign, this was her escape place. She had become very stubborn and would not listen to James when needing advice.

James said he would book the flights for Pimchan to fly to Thailand, but she wanted to do it herself, as she was particular which airline she would fly with, so it was left at that. She said he could do the return bookings. This was a big step for her as she and James always flew together and because her English was quite hard to understand, it was going to be a big undertaking. On the day she was due to fly out they drove three hours to the airport only to find the flight was cancelled. No one had rung to let them know! They then had to drive back home and return the next day.

At the airport James waited with Pimchan to see she got on her flight okay, as she was flying to Australia then on to Thailand. Because of the cancelled flight the day before she had missed her connecting flight to Thailand so the online travel agency rebooked her flights. James waited as Pimchan disappeared among the passengers waiting in line to go through customs. He stayed just to make sure all was fine. Then he noticed everyone had gone through except Pimchan, who was standing on her own. He asked to go through to see what was wrong. The customs lady told her she couldn't get on the plane as she didn't have a New Zealand passport so wasn't allowed into Australia. James told her this was not true as he knew from experience that because she would only be in the transit lounge, she was allowed to be there for four hours without a New Zealand passport. The customs lady went and checked and found out what James had told her was right, so now Pimchan could go through, as the plane was nearly ready to take off. This was sad for Pimchan as she couldn't explain herself in her pidgin English. He hoped from here on all was going to go okay for her. He drove three hours back to the farm.

Later that night he got a phone call from Pimchan and she was in tears. When she landed in Australia, she had two hours to board the next flight, but because the travel agency had changed her bookings, she went to the wrong airline counter and was told she wasn't booked on that particular flight. She was upset and she could not be understood, so by the time they got an interpreter and realised she was at the wrong counter, her plane had gone without her. Here she was in Australia not being allowed to be there for more than four hours, with no more flights to Thailand until seven o'clock the next evening. This was why she rung James, as they wanted an extra $450 to change her ticket. James told her not to pay any money, as he would sort it out with the travel agency. She was so distraught the airlines got her a temporary Australian visa, which allowed her to stay in Australia for three days. She couldn't afford to stay in a hotel so slept the night on the floor at the airport. James told her not to leave the airport the next day and just to hang around until her flight was due to go, as he didn't want her to miss another flight. He was worried for her. The next night she flew out to Thailand at seven o'clock and was due to arrive there at 5 am, so it meant she had to hang around the airport until she could catch a bus to Kantharalak. Poor Pimchan — she had lost two days and realised that to have had James with her would have been so much easier, as he understood what the requirements were regarding airports. Her so-called independence had not paid off. Next time James could do her bookings!

She had six days with her parents and to get Mali organised for her new life in New Zealand. The grandparents cried — they were sad to see Mali go, as she had lived with them for fourteen years. Also, did this mean no money would be forthcoming from Pimchan because Mali was not going to be there? This would be a huge worry for them. Lawana was now working in South Korea as a street vendor, selling food at night to passing travellers for a company, and on the odd occasion she didn't send money back for her children. The grandparents' life was falling apart because Pimchan had always been the one who sent money when it was asked for. Now things were going to be different. There was the expense of a school uniform for Mali and no one knew what lay ahead for Chai. As Mali was only fourteen, she would have to attend school in New Zealand until she was sixteen. But what of the language barrier? It was easier for Pimchan to brush this aside until she was confronted with this issue.

After leaving Kantharalak, she and Mali had to catch a bus to the other side of Bangkok where Chai was living, then they travelled down to the capital where they would stay the night before catching the plane the next morning. Pravat had signed all the necessary papers for Chai to go to New Zealand. This was going to be a totally new experience for these two teenagers. For years they had never lived more than two weeks at any one time with their mother or with each other as sister and brother, so they were leaving behind the only security they knew. For Mali it was going to be a huge step into the unknown as she was leaving behind her three cousins who she had lived with since she was a baby. Also leaving the communal village lifestyle that posed no restrictions for life on a rural farm situated twenty minutes from the nearest town.

The flight left Bangkok for Sydney in Australia then on to Christchurch, New Zealand, where they caught a domestic flight down south. They had been flying for fifteen hours so were utterly exhausted when James picked them up at the airport. He drove them home to the farm where they fell into their beds oblivious to the world outside. It was only the next day when they woke did it all start to sink in. For the first time Mali had her own bedroom. Pimchan and James had bought her a new queen bed, and put a desk in for her to use for whatever, hoping to make her feel welcome. Chai's life had not been as poor as that of his sister, therefore was used to having a room of his own.

The first barrier to try to overcome was that of language, as this left James on the outer. He asked them all to try to speak English as much as possible, but even after all the years Pimchan had lived in New Zealand her English had not improved. This was going to be problem number one! James had been in touch with the two colleges in the city but only one was interested in enrolling Mali. It was not the college of Pimchan's choice as she wanted her to attend a co-ed school, but really, there was no choice. James understood this, as Mali had very little knowledge of the English language, but Pimchan was not an easy person to reason with. They decided to wait for two weeks before they took Mali along to meet the headmistress of the girls' college as this would give the siblings time to get to know each other. The dairy farmer who both James and Pimchan worked for had offered Chai work on the farm. He was happy about this, as jobs in Thailand for him were practically non-existent. This was his chance to secure a future in a new country.

James had just given his notice to finish on the farm where he had been working for the last four years. The hours were long, from 4 am to 6 pm. He felt he was being taken advantage of, and was not afraid to speak out. This did not go down well with his boss; he was not used to a worker voicing his opinion. The reason being he hired foreign workers who came out on contract for two years and thcy could not have any opinions otherwise they would be sent back to their home country. Most at the end of their contract were happy to leave. He brought workers out from the Ukraine, India, France and the Philippines, but no one had lasted as long as James and Pimchan. As Pimchan was still the milking shed manager, they were entitled to stay in the farmhouse.

Each day James drove Chai into the city for two-hour English lessons at a special class so he could learn farming terms. This was organised by the agriculture sector for foreign workers, especially in the dairy industry. James was the only one in the family with a driving licence so he became the chauffeur. Next was to take Mali to the college to be assessed for her English, but when she was rated with a zero, the college refused to accept her. But as she had been granted New Zealand residency, she had to attend school until she was sixteen. A week later James and

Pimchan took her back to the school and it was agreed upon with the headmistress that Mali sit in on classes and observe. She would also be given an hour-long English lesson each day. For the next fortnight James drove Mali to school and picked her up when school finished each day, until she had the confidence to catch the school bus. The siblings had become firm friends and spent many hours on their computers, especially Mali, as she could be on Facebook with her friends back in Thailand, corresponding in the Thai language. English was not being spoken in the home, which disappointed James, as this had been discussed with Pimchan before the children arrived, but it was not being followed up on.

Chai had started on the farm and after receiving his first pay he was pleasantly surprised, as he thought the hourly rate quoted was what he earned for a full day's work, of course relating it back to Thai earnings. This gave him the incentive to want to work, as he could see the money he could make and save. Several months later the language barrier was still proving difficult, as following instructions was difficult for both him and the boss. It was now up to Chai to persevere and put in time to improve his English if he wanted to survive in the working environment. At the moment he is solely reliant on his mother to pass on instructions from the boss to him. This is not ideal as when they work different shifts, Pimchan has to be there to instruct him. He is earning good money and has bought himself all the latest electronic equipment, things he could never have afforded in Thailand. He bought his sister a new up-to-date phone, which was really nice. James tries to teach them to read and write in English at night but being teenagers and virtual strangers to him, he is finding he has no rights. He wants them to have the opportunity to make better lives for themselves in a country where everything is plentiful. Pimchan still crawls into her silent moods, which makes life difficult for them all at times. This is when it is easier for her to talk in Thai to her children, thus leaving James feeling he is not part of the family.

Four months have now passed and cracks are starting to appear! Pimchan and Mali's friendship has soured a little, as she will not discuss her schooling with her mother, thus leaving Pimchan in the dark. Mali spends many hours on Facebook, always corresponding in Thai with her friends. She has made friends with two Thai girls at college, which probably isn't going to help her English progress. Pimchan will not take the lead role of a parent with Mali, as she treats her as a friend. The rules that were first discussed have not been followed, as no English is being spoken in the home, leaving James frustrated, as these were not the terms discussed in the first place. This is where, as a mother, Pimchan has not enforced any rules on her children, so very little respect is shown. Her position as a mother has not materialised. There are no ground rules, they are treated more as friends than children, therefore they do their own thing without any thought for their mother or James. He cannot interfere, as this has been spelt out to him by Pimchan; they are her children.

Pimchan and James's lives have changed since the

arrival of the children. It was never easy before, but it has become a lot more complicated. All James wanted was to give the children the opportunity of a better life in a new country. Perhaps if this had all happened before they became teenagers, their ability to learn English may have been easier... who knows?

Chai is earning good money and is sending it home to his grandparents in Thailand, who are organising a home to be built for him. One day he will return and marry a Thai girl, as he is not interested in New Zealand girls. As a mother who lost touch with her son for so many years, Pimchan spoils him, trying to make up for their years apart, but those lost years can never be retrieved, they have passed. He has now been given a chance to make something of his life, but he will always be a Thai lad. One who is not prepared to adapt to the Kiwi way of life, therefore when it suits him, he will leave his mother and go back to his grandparents in Thailand. Meanwhile he will continue to treat James with contempt.

James has found a new job, one where he is his own boss. He always loved nature and the outdoors so now has become a possum trapper. The local farmers let him on their private reserves as they know he doesn't carry a gun so will not shoot their deer. He has one hundred traps and attends them every day. He loves his new job; at times it isn't easy lugging many traps at a time far into the bush, but he is rewarded for his hard work. Now that the weather is getting cooler and the berries and fruits from the forest are disappearing, the possums are seeking the bait from his traps, so his tally is steadily growing. The cooler the weather, the better quality the fur, which is worth from $120 to $130 a kilogram. The fur quantity and quality differ from one area to another. In cooler, damp areas there are about ten to twelve possums for a kilo of fur, but in drier, warm areas it takes from fifteen to eighteen possums to get a kilo. This leaves Pimchan and Chai working on the dairy farm and allows James time away. They still live in the farmhouse. James has never been happier; he is his own boss and escapes the Thai chatter until he returns.

Of course, there are going to be fallouts along the way, as neither James nor Pimchan are perfect, but in the end, respect must be given to the person who undertook to make a better life for these two siblings. Sadly, this has not happened. The big question being, will this marriage stand the test of time or will the children's attitude towards James drive them apart?

What does the future hold for this multicultural family? Only time will tell!

II

AMIRA — A KURDISH MILITANT

'Mountain Kurds': when their usefulness had run out, they were abandoned, their promises of a Kurdish state gone. Will they be 'forever refugees', America? You have done them wrong!

1

AMIRA'S BEGINNING

THE BOMBS WERE DROPPING NEARBY and the dust and smoke-filled air was choking us. Mother hid us under her dress, there was nowhere else to hide. All the buildings were crumbled ruins. These were once our homes, but no more; all that was left was rubble. We took shelter wherever, nowhere was safe any more. The terrorists had made sure nothing remained. We, the Kurds, meant nothing to them other than targets. Our people had no rights. Although we were a diverse race of people residing throughout many Middle Eastern countries, we had no identity.

For centuries our ancestors lived in the mountains, the high plains where Mesopotamia became Anatolia, with our own language, culture and identity. Our forebears led a nomadic life that revolved around sheep and goat farming. They lived in small villages in remote mountain regions. A typical Kurdish home was made of mud brick with a wooden roof. In summer, families slept on the roof where it was cooler. Some homes had underground rooms to be used in the winter to escape the cold. Rarely was there indoor plumbing, so water had to be carried in jars and cans from a central village well. Very few Kurds married non-Kurds. Kurdish culture had a rich, oral tradition, mostly epic poems telling of adventure in love or battle.

Mother feared for us three children. Our father had long gone, no one knew where; perhaps he had died fighting the terrorists alongside his countrymen. My brothers vowed they would fight as soon as they were old enough, much to the sadness of my mother. She didn't raise her boys to be lost fighting. Most of the other boys their age had joined the Kurdish fighters to try to save what was left of our city, but our fighters didn't have the warfare the opposing enemy had. I would lie awake at night and listen to my siblings talking brutal talk, about what they were going to do to the enemy. It sent shivers down my spine, but they were angry young men out for revenge! They had seen so much sadness, women and children lying dead among the ruins that were once their homes.

Food was scarce. We only ate what mother could salvage from the ruins along with hundreds of other mothers, as no shops had survived the bombing. The nights were cold so we all huddled together to keep warm. All the trees in the parks and gardens had been cut down for firewood, being the only source of warmth people had to survive. The land looked bare, as any vegetation that was useful had been taken. As darkness arrived, many families came together for shelter and comfort, as nowhere was safe any more. Bombs dropped and gunfire rang out day and night, so we never knew if we would wake up in the morning to live another day. Each day we saw civilians fleeing but many were caught up in the crossfire and lay wounded in the dust.

Today it was my best friend who lay wounded, so I ran to her and held her in my arms. We cried together. I couldn't let her go, she was my best friend, my only friend. We shared dreams of what life would be like one day, but now Arjen's dreams were ending along with her life. I felt her shaking violently as blood poured from her body. A piece of shrapnel had lodged in her chest, I knew the end was near. "Amira, my friend, seek revenge, promise me you will fight ISIS, save our people … please," then she fell silent. Arjen's request resonated in my heart along with our friendship. We buried her alongside all the other casualties, in the south corner of the park.

My brothers' hatred had turned into revenge for the bloodshed the terrorists had brought to our people. Because we were Kurds living in Turkey, we received unsympathetic treatment at the hands of the Government, who took away our identity by labelling us as 'Mountain Turks', outlawing the Kurdish language and not allowing us to wear our traditional dress. Even our Kurdish street names had to be taken down and disposed of. We were stripped of all we knew; we amounted to nothing in the eyes of those outside our culture. All Kurdish schools were shut down, and we found it impossible to attend schools that were foreign to all facets of our life. This was not us as we knew ourselves, we were being brainwashed to adjust to another culture, meaning we could no longer be ourselves! Many children never attended school, therefore the Kurdish literacy rate was very low, especially among the girls.

No wonder my brothers wanted revenge, but I had those very feelings myself, since losing my best friend. I missed her every day. One day I vowed to join the hundreds of young female Kurd soldiers and take up the fight against ISIS.

Mother tried to keep her three children together, but as the boys grew older, they developed minds of their own. She knew it would be only a matter of time before they left to join the Kurdish fighters. This happened sooner than anticipated. A few days later they made their big announcement: they were leaving and travelling to Syria, where they would join the Kurdish militants to help take down ISIS. Mother and I cried as we cuddled the boys. Would we ever see them again? How would we know if they were safe? But they were full of spirit and enthusiasm; this was their calling, to make a better life for the remaining Kurds. "Mother, our lives are worthless here. If we don't help our countrymen, we will never belong anywhere. We deserve better than what we have, we are just refugees without a country of our own. No one wants us. One day we must belong somewhere!" The family said their goodbyes among tears. Was this their last meeting?

Through the underground movement the boys heard Turkey had renewed its crackdown on the PKLG (aligned Kurds), who were strengthening their self-governance in northeastern Syria amid the continued civil war of Syria and the fight against the Islamic state of Iraq. Also, the Kurds felt strong assimilationist pressure from the national government in Iran, and endured religious prosecution by that country's Muslim majority. Now was the best time to act! As the boys travelled by bus to Syria, they passed graveyards which held some of the 60,000 Kurds killed by Saddam Hussein's forces. Concrete ruins marked the remains of homes destroyed in waves of battles against ISIS, in which the Kurds of both Iraq and Syria fought to the death. This did not deter the boys. They were on their way to do battle; it was the hatred they harboured in their hearts that was the driving force for them to join their fellow countrymen.

2

A TIMELY DEATH!

MEANWHILE, Amira and her mother's lives were filled with fear and hatred. The bombing was still happening and with each new day came death and destruction. Young children were leaving the safety of their remaining family members to scout for food, as they were starving, and they were the unlucky ones that were caught up in the crossfire, leaving many of them dead and wounded. Nothing could be done to help the wounded; they just lay in their mothers' arms until they passed away. Such sadness surrounded these people; it was a battle of heroic proportions just to stay alive. Amira cried herself to sleep most nights while lying in her mother's arms, thinking of her friend Arjen, who knew nothing other than bombs and crossfire. They would never experience their dreams together, the ones they shared, the ones that kept a smile on their young faces until that fateful day when all their dreams were taken from them. It was on that day Amira's smiles ceased, and instead a sadness crept in and never left.

The days came and went, nothing changed. It was a matter of survival — to stay alive, to find food so they didn't starve. Amira was now fifteen. She was a pretty girl, which drew glances from the opposite sex, but she didn't know in her own heart that this was happening; she was oblivious to what was going on around her. All her love was for her mother, who she worried about as she wasn't well. It was her time to leave her mother's side and go to search for food. While doing this she resorted to begging from the soldiers as they always had food, but they weren't the nicest of men, expecting something in return, in other words, favours! This was when the 'touching' started. First it was her breasts. They all lined up and asked her to take off her top. She didn't want to do this, but her mother needed food. Then they all squeezed her breasts with their rough hands, laughing and joking among themselves, but all the time hurting Amira. She closed her eyes and wished it would stop, but the thought of starvation was worse than what was happening to her.

Two days passed before Amira had to go and find more food as her mother was very weak. She dreaded going back to the soldiers to beg for food, but she had no choice. The love for her mother was far stronger than any thought of what the soldiers might want. This time it was different: one lone soldier pulled her into the ruins and started kissing her in a brutal manner holding her tightly to his body. He then slipped a hand inside her knickers touching her private parts and hurting her. She tried to break free but she couldn't escape his firm grasp, so she started to cry and it was only then he released her. He gave her his lunchbox and she took off back to her mother. Next time he would not be so lenient on her; she would have to supply more than a mere touch for his next lunchbox. Amira would make sure this food lasted at least two days, as she did not want to go back near those horrible men ever again.

During the night Amira could feel her mother shaking and she was complaining that she was cold, when in fact she had a fever. She cuddled into her, frightened to think what might be wrong. Nothing could happen to her, she was her only family, her only love, in fact she was her everything. What would life be like without her mother? There would be nothing, only emptiness. She could not think of life beyond her. Amira drifted off to sleep and awoke in the morning to the feeling of a cold stillness, a feeling that was foreign to her. What did it mean? There was no warmth from her mother. "Mother, wake up, are you sick?" she called, but no reply was forthcoming. It was only then she realised her mother's body was cold and stiff. She had seen this many times before and only now realised what had happened. She lay beside her sobbing, "Please don't leave me, mother, I'm all alone, I have no one!" but it was all in vain, she knew her mother had died. Nothing could change what had happened, it was irreversible. She lay next to her mother praying for a miracle, but these never happened; one could only dream of them, but, in reality, they never materialised.

People nearby heard her sobs and came to see if Amira was all right. It was only then they realised the 'Almighty' had again visited them and claimed yet another victim. They lifted Amira up and took her aside while others attended to her mother. Because no one knew what had caused her death, it was best to bury her as soon as possible, before any diseases broke out, so they set about digging a grave. Amira watched as her mother was laid to rest, then she sank down on her knees and prayed endlessly for the only love she had ever known, apart from her best friend Arjen. What of her brothers? Would they be sad to hear of their mother's death? But death was part of everyday life here, it was not an uncommon occurrence to have to bury many bodies each day. Everyone had suffered, it showed on their faces, but life had to go on for those left behind.

Now that Amira was on her own, her grief never went away — it lingered on, as she loved her mother dearly and, along with Arjen, nothing else mattered in her world. Arjen had been robbed of a future, not that it looked at all bright; all Amira could see ahead was gloom. Her two loves had been taken from her. What next?

Meanwhile back at the fighting front, a soldier was waiting for the young girl to turn up to beg for his lunch. He liked what he had seen and touched, and now his mind was set on taking more from her. She was young and innocent and he was excited by this. It was a long time since he had been home to his wife, so the thoughts of a young girl conjured up an excitement that he couldn't wait to release. Several days had passed and she had not turned up, which left him wondering, what could be wrong? But he held on to his fantasies, reliving them time and time again. All that had to happen was for her to appear!

Her mother's timely death had certainly saved Amira from having her innocence stolen by a merciless soldier. Did her mother sense something, or was someone above looking out for her? Was it an act of God?

It took several months before Amira could tear herself away from her mother's resting place. She had sat for days thanking her mother for telling her stories of the sad life the Kurdish people had endured and how the future looked bleak. They were a very diverse community, settling in many countries, some of which treated them okay, but other countries wanted rid of them. What they wanted and were promised was a Kurdish state that they could call home, where peace and happiness could be restored in their hearts. But as yet this hadn't happened. Now her thoughts switched to her brothers; all she knew was they had crossed over the border to Syria, where they wanted to become militant fighters. She had nothing to keep her in Turkey. Her heart was telling her to take revenge on Arjen's murderers, Arjen's last request, so she would remain true to her promise. It was time to go!

3

SEEKING SWEET REVENGE

AMIRA WAS TAKING the same journey as her brothers to cross into Syria, so she saw the same devastation as they had. It tugged at her heart. How could people be so merciless to so many others? But then she only had to look at her own life and it all came flooding back. The Kurds were unwanted people; they were commonly known as 'Mountain Kurds' with no state of their own. The greatest problem for the Kurds was the unwillingness of nations in which they lived to give them cultural independence. Most Kurds are Sunni Muslims (a branch of Islam), only about one fifth are Shiite Muslims who live in Iran. In their culture they marry young, about seventeen and eighteen, and marriage between first cousins is common. A man often marries the daughter of one of his father's brothers. They are a very family-orientated race of people.

As Amira crossed into Syria she felt alone and frightened. She had no idea where her brothers were, or anything about them, and wondered if they would be sad when they learnt of their mother's death. She would have to make enquiries as to where the Kurdish guerrilla fighters were based and then work from there. She knew it would be dangerous, but she was ready, as she had nothing to live for! She had lost the two dearest people in her life. What did she have left? Just an empty heart, which was now savaged by revenge. On the bus in the seat in front of her were two young men talking about joining the guerrilla fighters. Were they Kurds? she asked herself, so she leaned forward and asked them who they were fighting for. They were taken by surprise. Who was this young girl asking questions, was she friend or foe? Amira explained that she was going to join her brothers and become a guerrilla fighter and fight for the rights of the Kurdish people. One of the young lads told her not to be so forthcoming with that sort of information, as it could put her life in danger, but to her delight, they were two Kurdish lads with the same thoughts as her. A three-way conversation began between them, thus making her feel a little safer and less vulnerable. They asked about her brothers but she couldn't tell them much, as she had had no contact with them since they left a year ago. The lads had a rough idea where the guerrillas were based, as that was where they were heading. "Can you take me with you?" she asked. The lads didn't know how to answer this, as they themselves didn't know what was going to greet them, so they left the question unanswered. Amira knew not to push this matter any further at the moment, for fear they would abandon her, thus meaning she might never meet up with her brothers.

They reached Syria late at night so the lads asked Amira to shelter with them, as they felt sad for her being on her own in a strange country. For this she was very grateful. They discussed between themselves about taking her with them to the military base, but felt it might be unsafe for her among so many fighting men. They had dossed down in a bus shelter for the night and this was the first time in months that Amira felt safe, so she slept right through the night. She was woken the next morning by the lads who had been told where the guerrillas were based, but it was a long steep hike, so perhaps it would be better if she didn't come. This brought on a protest: "I have to come and find my brothers, they are all I have left!" she sobbed.

Nothing more was said, so the three of them set off on the long, uphill journey. The climb nearly killed Amira but she battled on; no way could she let the lads down. It took most of the day to reach the camp, and they were met with a strict entry procedure. One could only enter on the basis that they knew someone in the camp, as an identity confirmation. This was so no enemy infiltrated their camp. The lads knew no one so Amira told them she had two brothers in the camp who were Kurdish militants. They took her brothers' names and told them to wait. It seemed like hours instead of minutes, when suddenly before her stood her eldest brother, Amed. The tears flowed as they hugged each other. "What are you doing here, Amira?" She told him their mother had passed away and now she had no one except her brothers, so had made up her mind that she wanted to fight for a new Kurdish state. "Where is Behaz?" she asked. "We lost him. A group of ISIS guerrillas took some of our men in an ambush. We have not seen them again so we don't know if they are dead or alive," he sobbed. The two siblings shared their grief; now they only had each other.

"But you cannot stay here, Amira, this is a camp for men who are prepared to put their lives out there. Many are not of good character, they are rough and uncouth. You must leave here immediately. If you want to become a guerrilla fighter and take up the fight against ISIS, join the hundreds of young female soldiers. They are part of the YPJ or Women's Protection Unit, an offshoot of the Kurdish Workers' Party," he explained to her. The PKK, a Kurdish nationalist movement, had long fought a war of independence against Turkey. The desire to break free from the macho Middle East was so strong, the rural girls volunteered to join the YPJ and put their lives on the line. "This is where you must go. You must leave here, it is too dangerous for a young woman," he pleaded with her. "But I can't go back on my own," she said. Amed arranged for a young soldier, a friend of his, to deliver her back to the nearest town and gave her all the information she needed on where to find the YPJ movement. Amira hugged her brother. Was this the final farewell or would they meet again? She told him she loved him amid her sobs. Now it was time for her to depart as the young man wanted to get on his way, with darkness descending. This was a dangerous time to be out in the mountains; they must leave immediately. Amed tore himself free from Amira's arms and said, "Keep safe, my little sister, I'm proud of you. Whatever happens I will always treasure this moment." Then he disappeared.

4

LIFE AS A GUERRILLA

AMIRA HAD FOUND her way to Til Kocher, with much help from the young man her brother had entrusted her to. She was made welcome by the women militants. Their headquarters was an abandoned apartment building, just one of many that had been partly destroyed during the bombing of the city. It was a neglected area; this was the perfect hideaway for these young women fighters. In another part of the bombed-out building was their arsenal of weapons, ranging from American M4 rifles and locally manufactured .50 calibre sniper rifles. These women belonged to the YPJ militia, a military force of trained citizens for use in emergency only, and were helping out in the fight against ISIS in northern Syria. They were drawn into battle when they learned of ISIS murdering Kurdish children. This they deemed an emergency.

It didn't take long before Amira was indoctrinated into the world of fighting. There were children from the age of ten years old, and women into their sixties, all there for a common cause, to take out ISIS. Her first job as a new recruit was to help remove rubble and make a clear area so they could dig long narrow trenches in which they threw the bodies of the ISIS guerrillas that they had shot. There was no mercy shown towards the enemy, as this was payback for the hideous crimes they had committed on the Kurdish people. Hiding the bodies was to safeguard themselves, because if the enemy saw that so many of their fighters' bodies lay in the trenches, it would have been certain death, and terrible ones at that for the women. They all knew the risks they were taking, but these young and older women had lost most of those close to them, so, like Amira, they decided if they could make a better life for other Kurds, then to give up one's life was the price they were prepared to pay.

At night they would sit on the rubble and each would tell of the horrors that had confronted them, so they all had a similar understanding of what their cause was … to rid ISIS at any cost. Amira soon learnt these women meant business. They had an incentive system of sorts for their snipers. Sidearms were a prized possession on the battlefield and snipers who achieved twenty kills received a Makarov pistol. Once they had killed over one hundred ISIS snipers, they were awarded a Beretta pistol. This was the ultimate weapon, and to achieve this, one had to be very brave as well as an excellent shot. Amira had never used a rifle before, so began her lessons. In between times she was on the task of dragging bodies to the trenches they had dug.

She had no remorse for these men. Her memory went back to the soldiers she had to beg food from and the laughing and joking as they squeezed her breasts, hurting her. Then her last day of begging when she was accosted by the soldier who had pulled her hard against him and touched a private part of her body. It made her shudder. It was only then she realised that she had been spared a worse fate by the death of her mother. Did her mother give up her life so Amira didn't have to suffer further at the hands of these ruthless men?

Today was Amira's first day on the battlefield. She had spent the last fortnight practising with a rifle and had impressed her leader, so now had come the time for her to shoot her first ISIS militant. A group of ten guerrilla women made their way to where the gunfire was coming from and settled into position. They could see several ISIS soldiers advancing towards them, so they waited for the command to shoot to be given, then they let fire. Three men fell to the ground but one escaped. They had to find him before he alerted others in his party as to their whereabouts. Nasiba, who was the commander, told them to stay and she would hunt him down. Suddenly she signalled to Amira to follow her. The two of them climbed among the ruins until they spotted the escapee. "You take him, Amira," she commanded. Amira lifted her rifle and pulled the trigger and down he went. As they got close to him, they realised he was only wounded. Nasiba pulled a knife from her waist and gave it to Amira, telling her to finish him off. She had never killed anyone before, but to be part of the organisation one had to obey orders. Suddenly her memory went back to when her friend lay dying in her arms, asking her to seek revenge, and this was all it took. She held the knife above his heart and lunged forward. "Die, you bastard! This is for you, Arjen, my promise to you I have kept. Rest in peace, my dear friend," then she cheered loudly. "I hope you are listening, Jihadists, this is your worst nightmare, to be taken down by a woman!" Nasiba looked on in disbelief. Here was a new recruit and she had carried out her command without a protest and showed no remorse; this was the making of a good soldier! She would keep her eye on her.

Amira dragged the body over the rubble and back to the trench, where she pushed it over the side to where all the other bodies lay. Each night they would throw dirt and debris into the trench just enough to cover those that lay there. When the trench was full, they would cover it with large pieces of rubble so no one would ever know what lay beneath! Then on they went to the next one.

Kurdish women did not boast about their kills in combat, perhaps because it was their belief that they were fighting for Kurdish freedom. They were heroes fighting a ruthless war with no logistical support, no air support, obsolete weapons and equipment and no medical back-up. They fought a barbaric horde of Islamic militants and when they died, no one cared. These are the heroic, the brave, but unlike American heroes they receive no accolades, no medals, and displays of courage to the public were not on their agenda. They were there to do a job and they knew what was expected of them … rid Syria of ISIS!

Today was a sad day as two of her comrades had not returned; were they dead or had they been taken prisoners? These were sad moments for the group, as they all knew what fate awaited women fighters, so they had to regroup and support each other. It was like losing a family member, but it was always on the cards and this was a grave reminder! Tonight, a meeting was called, as a vital piece of information had reached them. Nasiba, the commander, stood up and spoke. "I will be taking five comrades with me tomorrow and we will be following ISIS soldiers to see where they are going to station themselves. We will not shoot; this is a surveillance exercise. We have to know their location, as we are the closest militia, then this information will be forwarded on to the PKK [aligned Kurds] who in turn will deal to them. It is too dangerous for us to handle." Nasiba named the five comrades and Amira was surprised when her name was called out. She felt honoured. Tomorrow at dawn they would leave, as they had been tipped off in what direction the ISIS snipers were thought to be heading, but it needed to be verified. This would be a three-day mission, and guns would be carried but hopefully not used.

The comrades walked in single file towards the mountains, aware that at all times they had to be vigilant. It was not an easy walk as the undulating ground did not help their cause. It would take them a full day of hiking to get to the vantage point they were briefed on. Just on darkness they reached their destination, so set up camp. They were perched on a high point and had a full view of the surrounding land; anyone passing through would not escape their attention. This meant a 24-hour watch, so they had to take turns. If the ISIS militants came through during the night, their lights would be a dead giveaway. This meant they would pack up their tents and move with them, so they were prepared to move at a moment notice. Their job was to establish where ISIS were going to set up base camp, then they would get a message through to the PKK who in turn would attack. This was only one of the ISIS cells, but to rid one, was one less to torture the Kurdish people.

It was early morning that the army of ISIS was spotted making their way to their next destination. Much to the surprise of the YPJ, many of the men were unarmed. They were carrying packs and looked like ordinary people looking to settle in a new area. Was this a ploy? The Kurdish women spread out and worked their way along the ridges in single file, mapping out the ISIS route. It was thought they would set up camp on the outskirts of the next village, hoping to take the Kurdish people by surprise. But this was not their motive. They had instituted a policy of settling Iraqi Arabs in areas with Kurdish majorities, let them mingle with the people, then when the time was right, they would bring in their reinforcements and wipe them out.

As was expected, the ISIS militants made camp in the remains of several bomb shelters on the outskirts of the town, so as not to draw attention to themselves. This mission was now completed for the Kurdish women, so they made their way back to headquarters, so as to get a message back to the PKK. For this attack to be successful the PKK would have to act immediately, before ISIS infiltrated their spies into the town. This plan was not known to either of the Kurdish militant camps. It took several days before the PKK attacked and killed most of the unsuspecting ISIS snipers, but was it too late? How many men were now infiltrated into the Kurdish community?

5

A NEW LOCATION FOR AMIRA

Two years on, with the battles still raging, Amira was told she was needed in a new location, at Kirkuk, in Iraq, near the Iranian border. Thousands of Kurds had fled to Iran and Turkey. Kirkuk, an oil-rich city, had a Kurd majority, but they were being uprooted from these regions. This policy had accelerated in the 1980s as large numbers of Kurds were forcibly relocated particularly from areas along the Iranian border where Iraqi authorities suspected the Kurds were aiding Iranian forces during the Iran-Iraqi war in 1980–88. The fighting was still ongoing years later so this was where Amira was needed, along with ten other Kurdish militants from their headquarters. Word was out that Iraqi forces were using large quantities of chemical warfare on Kurdish civilians to quell Kurdish resistance. This was one of the most brutal episodes in Kurdish history. Innocent women and children lay dying, choking on the gases from these weapons. Amira and her comrades were outraged by this barbaric act, so retaliation was first and foremost on their minds. They entered the city to find piles of corpses, many of them children, all waiting to be buried. They had dug trenches before, so helped the grieving family members who had survived to bury their loved ones. Now it was revenge: all ISIS snipers must be killed; they would pick them off one by one.

It wasn't hard to find ISIS snipers, as they hid in ruins but were proud to have their distinctive flag flying. Amira and her comrades had joined up with a large YPJ women's group, so now they were a force to be reckoned with. They would wait until the snipers opened fire, then they would retaliate. This area was different from their last posting — they didn't have to hide the bodies, as they lay everywhere and no one cared! By now she had a good eye for her targets, as she had worked her way up to using a Beretta. She had shot over two hundred enemy. She had no remorse; a dead ISIS soldier was another notch on her belt and she had many more to collect.

They would not leave wounded ISIS snipers, they would finish them off; they carried knives for that very reason. The only time remorse took over Amira was when one of her comrades was badly wounded and they had to kill her, so she would not be left at the mercy of the guerrillas. It was a rule and they all knew it had to be abided by. Sad as it was, it had to happen.

Their YPJ group had received word that one of the largest chemical attacks took place on 16 March in the village of Halabjah, when Iraqi troops killed as many as

5000 Kurds with mustard gas and nerve agent. This was cause for Amira and a large group of their fighters to go there and join other offshoots of their organisation to help with casualties and rise against the enemy. The city was in shambles; graves needed to be dug to bury the dead, so this was their first deployment. The women were reduced to tears to see so many innocent civilians, particularly children, whose lives had been stolen from them, almost before they had begun. The YPJ movement were hardcore fighters, but nothing could stop the heartache that faced them. Their feelings were expressed in their tears. But still ISIS and Iraqi troops attacked the city and killed more civilians. Would this ever stop?

At night Amira and her comrades scouted the city hoping to pick off enemy snipers. They always went in pairs for safety's sake. Tonight was different; the city had an unusual silence. What did this mean? It didn't take long to find out, as missiles landed all around, sending people scattering for their lives. The YPJ went into action. Bullets were coming in all directions, so the group split up to find where the main ISIS threshold was. When they found the main battle source, they opened fire on their enemy, hoping to take many out. Crossfire raged for hours until Amira's world descended into darkness.

6

THE YOUNG DOCTOR

WHEN SHE WOKE, she was lying in a hospital bed. She had no idea what she was doing there, although she could feel pain in her upper body. She could hear screaming all around her and hospital staff were running everywhere. More civilians had been shot and needed immediate treatment, thus why the hospital was so busy. As she went to sit up, she felt pain in her right shoulder and then realised it was bandaged. "You must lie still, you were shot in the shoulder, don't try to move." Standing beside her was a young male doctor. "What happened?" she asked. "You were brought in by members of the YPJ. Are you one of them?" Amira told him she had been with them for the past four years. "You are a very brave young woman. What makes you want to become a militant?" he enquired. She explained how many of her comrades had lost most of their family members to ISIS, or had been treated badly by enemy snipers. "What about yourself, what was your reason?" Amira told him how she had encountered ruthless men while having to beg for food for her sick mother. The doctor was intrigued and upset at the same time.

Why did these young women have to suffer so much? he asked himself. "You rest and I will be back tonight to check on you," and with this he left.

Amira felt sad as he walked away; what a pleasant young man. She didn't want him to leave, it was as if she had known him forever! Why did she feel this way? It had never happened before, but then she hadn't known many young men. As she looked around, she was horrified to see many bodies with severe burns. Was this the reason for the screaming? And still more people were being brought in. There didn't seem to be enough staff to attend to all these patients. As she lay there, her thoughts went back to her comrades — were they all okay? If she had been shot, who else was no longer part of their sisterhood? Hopefully someone would visit her and let her know what had happened, as she was still in the dark. With these thoughts, she drifted off to sleep.

"Wake up, Amira, let me look at your shoulder," and there before her was the young doctor. She rubbed her eyes and went to sit up but he gently held her down. "Just you lie there, I will remove the bandages and see how your wound is." He leaned over and removed the bandages then gently touched all around her shoulder area. What gentle hands; she had never been touched so tenderly by anyone other than her mother. Amira couldn't help but speak out. "You have such a gentle touch." The young doctor smiled and winked at her. There was something about this brave young militant that struck a chord with him. He felt an instant attraction, but he was the doctor and she was his patient, he had to remind himself, and that was the way it had to stay. He reapplied the bandage and patted her hand and said he would see her tomorrow, then he disappeared. Again, Amira felt sad, but why? She couldn't understand what was happening to her. Her heart ached when her thoughts turned to him, she didn't even know his name. She was just one of his many patients, she told herself.

Today she had visitors, as some of her comrades came to see how she was. "What happened? How did I get wounded?" she asked. It was then she learnt that the enemy snipers had opened fire in their direction all together, taking them by surprise. Her comrade did not survive; she had received a bullet through her chest, killing her instantly. Amira was shot in the shoulder but managed to hide until another of her comrades carried her back to their camp. This brought tears to her eyes; she had lost another friend to ISIS snipers. Was this ever going to end, or were they never going to give up until they had annihilated all the Kurds?

But with this sad news came an announcement that the United States of America were joining up with the Kurds, and would act as their allies against ISIS. The Kurds' reputation for military prowess made them much in demand as mercenaries for American forces. When her visitors left, Amira burst into tears. Why did her comrade have to die? They both wanted to work together and take out more ISIS soldiers, they were a team, but sadly no more! This was the heartbreak that came with being a sniper; there were no guarantees!

She buried her head under her pillow and sobbed, she felt so emotional. Was her guerrilla prowess leaving her, or were her emotions brought to the fore because of her feelings for the young doctor? She was a stranger to herself, which left her confused. "Hi, Amira, how are you today?" It was then the doctor noticed her tear-stained face. "What is wrong?" She told him her comrade had died and she had lived, and for this she felt guilty. "But you have survived, for that you must be thankful. You are lucky you arrived with relatively minor injuries. Look at all these other poor people who have been burnt by chemical warfare; this is when life isn't fair. I applaud your movement, you are the heroic ones, trying to make the world a safer place." These were words of comfort and Amira wanted to thank him for being so understanding. "Doctor, I am grateful for your kind words. I have never been spoken to like this before by a man." "Then you haven't met the right man," was his answer. "I'll be back before I finish tonight, see you then," and he was gone. That empty feeling had again visited her on his departure.

Yes, he was definitely affecting the way she thought, as well as messing with her feelings, but why? She had never thought about love, it hadn't entered her mind until now. Is this the effect it had on people? Was she experiencing love for the first time? Later that night, just as Amira was about to drop off to sleep, she felt a hand on her shoulder shaking her. "Wake up, Amira, I have to change your dress-ing," and there stood her doctor. "I won't be here tomor-row, so I will check this now, just to see if the healing process is doing its job." Her heart sank, she wouldn't see him tomorrow. Perhaps he was married. She just had to ask. "Do you have a wife and family?" "No, I am single. I haven't met the right person yet, but I am hoping it will happen soon, otherwise I will be an old man," he said with a smile. This sent warm shivers through her body, Did he sense that she liked him? "I have to operate at another hospital, as they are short of surgeons. We can't keep up with all the casualties that arrive every day, and we have a shortage of nursing staff, so everyone works long hours. I am hoping to discharge you within three days, but you will not be able to use a rifle for two months." "But I have upscaled to a pistol, I have served my apprenticeship. I have killed over two hundred ISIS militants, so that puts me in the pistol bracket," she said with a cheeky grin. "Then that puts any thoughts of being alone with you at night, out of the question," came back his answer. His hands moved gently over her shoulder, asking if there was any pain. He knew when she flinched that it was still tender. "You are a good healer, but we have to watch for infection. Please keep this area covered at all times until the wound heals. I will be back the day after tomorrow, so take care of yourself," then he was gone.

That night Amira cried herself to sleep. She wanted to feel his arms around her, to have him lying beside her so she could feel his warmth and his love. Just these thoughts sent tingling sensations through her body. She remembered her mother's love and the warmth it brought.

Today was the day her favourite doctor would be back, so she got out of bed and attempted to shower herself and give her hair a quick wash, which was difficult with one hand. Then she dressed. Stirring in the bed next to her was a young girl in tears, so she went over to see if she could be of any help. "I want someone to read me a story, I miss my mother," she said. Amira knew this feeling only too well! "Would you like me to read to you? I will find a book, then I'll sit on your bed with you." She went to a locker at the end of the ward and there were some pretty shabby books, but a story was a story, no matter where it came from. The young girl asked Amira why she was in hospital. When she told her she was a sniper, she was in awe. "You must be so brave. Perhaps one day that is what I might be." It was time to start reading and take her mind away from warfare. Smiles soon replaced the tears from an otherwise sad young face. "I can't read, I never went to school because they closed all our schools," she said. "Are you Kurdish?" Amira asked. This brought a nod of her head.

This was how the doctor found his favourite patient, perched on the young girl's bed bringing a little joy to the sad little soul who had lost both parents. He came over to Amira and smiled at her. "I see you have made a new friend." "Yes, I am reading her a story as she is missing her mother, so I will read until her mother arrives," she answered in all innocence, not knowing the girl was now an orphan. The doctor didn't say anything to the contrary, he wanted them to have a few moments of happiness together, as the young girl didn't know of the pending sadness she was going to have to face. He was dreading to have to tell her, but here was this friendly soul that had befriended her; perhaps she was the one to break the sad news? It looked like Amira had won her confidence, so yes, he would speak to her when she finished reading.

He went away to attend to other patients, leaving Amira a little sad as she had not had time to speak with him on her own. The young girl sensed something was wrong. "Why are you sad now?" she asked. Poor Amira didn't think it was that obvious. Innocently she shared her thoughts about the doctor with her. "Don't worry, he will be back," she commented. The storytelling continued.

Several hours passed before she saw the doctor again. First, he visited the young girl, who couldn't wait to do a little matchmaking. "That lady likes you; she was sad when you left. Is she your girlfriend?" "Not at the moment, but perhaps one day. She seems a nice young lady, don't you think?" he asked. "Yes, she is very brave. Do you know she is a guerrilla sniper? Isn't that exciting? I told her that is what I might be one day, but first I would have to ask my mother." Just the mention of the word 'mother' deflated him; she would have to be told soon.

He made his way to Amira's bed. "I see you have made a firm friend. She thinks you are very brave; you are her hero. There is something I want you to do for me. It will be sad, but you are the only person she has confided in since being here." Amira's heart fluttered, of course she would do anything for the doctor. It was only in this moment in time, she realised that she had fallen in love with him; he could ask anything of her. "The young girl lost both her parents in a missile attack, but she hasn't been told yet. I think you are the right person to break this sad news to her. Please will you tell her?" What a shock, how could she be the bearer of such sad news? They had just become friends, now this?" "Oh my God, what am I going to say?" she asked. "I will leave it in your hands. You have suffered also, so you both have something in common. I know I can rely on you, please do this for me?" She looked into his eyes and yes, there were tears. Amira knew this was important to him, and somehow she would do as he had requested. "Leave it to me," she consoled him. He squeezed her hand letting her know he was grateful, then he went on his way.

Tonight was the night the young girl would learn she no longer had a mother or a father. Amira was upset, but she had a promise to keep. She walked over and sat on her bed and took her hand. "What is wrong, Amira?" She had sensed something sad had happened; perhaps the doctor didn't like her! "I have sad news for you. You are in hospital because a missile hit where your family were hiding. You are the lucky one; you survived, but your mother and father have both died. Someone pulled you away but it was too late to save the others, I'm so sorry." The shocked look on her face said it all. Amira took her in her arms and held on to her while she sobbed her heart out. What on earth was going through her mind? She was only a young girl, fancy having to be told the worst possible news. "What will happen to me now?" she asked. Amira's arms never let go of her; she didn't know how to answer this question. They stayed wrapped in each other's arms until an announcement was made. "Take me with you, Amira, I want to become a sniper so I can revenge my parents' killers," then the sobbing started again. Was this a spur-of-the-moment decision or was she serious? Amira knew the feeling, as this is how she felt after her friend was taken, but she had to work through her pain before making any decisions.

The next morning Amira was still asleep when she was again woken by the doctor. "Wake up, sleepyhead." She opened her eyes and there he stood. She had to pinch herself to see if she wasn't still dreaming, as he had lain with her all night in her dreams. "How did your talk go?" he wanted to know. She told him what had happened and the outcome. "She asked what will happen to her now, do you know?" "As she has no family members alive, I guess when her legs are healed, she will live among the ruins like many others," he answered. "She mentioned about becoming a sniper. How old is she?" "I have her listed as ten years old, whether that is true, I don't know. I would like to repay you for helping me out. Would you like to come to my place and I will cook you dinner? I am discharging you tomorrow, so will tomorrow night be okay?" Amira hadn't even thought about life after leaving the hospital. Where would she go? She couldn't go back to headquarters as it was a bombed-out apartment, where they lived pretty rough, as did most militants. These were women with nothing other than comradeship.

Today was discharge day. Amira went and broke the news to Roserin, the girl in the bed next to her. "Please don't forget me. Come and see me, you are my only friend. Remember, when I am better, I want to be a sniper," she pleaded. "I want you to think seriously about this while you are recovering, then if you still feel the same, I will see what I can arrange," Amira told her. Age was no barrier, as many young girls were orphaned and wanted to become fighters. They didn't attend school, there was no Kurdish education, as it had been banned. So revenge played a big part in their lives, simply because ISIS had robbed them of their families. It was an exciting prospect for them. God knows they needed something to give them hope for the future!

7

AFTER THE DINNER

Amira wasn't leaving hospital until nearer the end of the day, so she sat with Roserin and they talked about the life of a sniper. She didn't post a rosy picture, she told it as it was. Their living conditions were pitiful, but this went with the territory, as they moved around a lot. It was not a glamour job, far from it. It was tonight she was going to the young doctor's place for dinner. She thanked her lucky stars she had access to a shower at the hospital. Then a thought crossed her mind: she didn't even know his name. How strange to be having dinner with someone without a name. She was so excited, she had to scold herself for being so emotional, but her feelings were getting the better of her, in fact they were nearly uncontrollable. The pair had agreed to meet at the front entrance of the hospital, then they would walk to his place together.

There he was waiting for her. She was in her military clothing, as that was all the soldier girls wore. They were militants first and foremost! "Hello, Amira, I'm looking forward to tonight," he greeted her. "Yes, I am too," was all she could get out, as she suddenly found herself tongue-tied. They walked side by side in silence until they arrived at an apartment block that had so far escaped the bombs. "Gosh, you live close to the hospital. Is that why the buildings have been spared?" "I'm not sure, but many hospital staff live here. It is convenient, as we are often called out at night to attend emergencies." "That must be hard at times, not to know if you can get a full night's sleep?" she asked. "It is my calling, as is yours. You try to take out ISIS and I patch up the damage they do to our people. We both dedicate our lives to what we believe in. Perhaps with the Kurds becoming allies with the American troops, we might see a light at the end of a long dark tunnel. We couldn't do it on our own; this may be the turning point."

In all her excitement, she realised she still didn't know his name, but as they entered the apartment, she saw the name 'Dr Beyani' on his door, so now she knew. The apartment was quite clinical, but this was understandable for a male on his own who probably spent more time at the hospital than in his home. He invited her to sit down while he went and changed from his hospital uniform. Amira looked around and saw a family photo on the wall, which she presumed was his family. The two children were very young, so she didn't know if her thoughts told her the truth.

Beyani offered her a drink, which she accepted. She had never consumed alcohol before, but she didn't want to let him know of her innocence. He brought over a glass, then sat down beside her. "I admire what you do, Amira, you are putting your life on the line to help save our people. That makes you a brave woman, but you are still young. Do you not want something different from life, something more fulfilling for yourself?" Amira thought for a moment; all she had on her mind was revenge on ISIS for having taken her friend, and for her missing brother. Personal wants had not been on her list, they had only just surfaced since meeting the doctor. She wondered how she was going to answer this. "I haven't thought much about my life, others have always come first." He leaned over and took her hand. "Amira, you must give yourself time or life will pass you by. We only get one life." She looked into his eyes and her heart melted. If she could be granted one wish, it would be to lie beside him and feel his warm body close to hers.

He let go of her hand and offered her another drink, while he went and attended to dinner. She didn't realise she had finished her first one but the glass was empty, so he refilled it. Amira's heart was racing. She sipped away at the second glass and before she knew, it was also empty. Her cheeks were burning and funny things were happening inside her body. Never before had she felt this vulnerable. She picked up her glass and walked over to the bottle and poured herself another drink, then walked back and sat down. As she was sipping away, Beyani called for her to come and be seated for dinner.

As she rose from her chair and went to walk towards the dining table, her legs were wobbly. Was something wrong with her? She called out, "Beyani, please help me, I can't walk straight," then the tears started. He took one look at her and realised what was wrong. "Have you drunk alcohol before?" "No, this is the first time. I helped myself to another glass from the bottle, was that wrong of me?" she asked as her legs gave out and she sank to the floor. He bent down and lifted her up. She looked so sad and help-less; her innocence tugged at his heart. Here was this brave soldier reduced to tears, simply because she had over-indulged in a little alcohol, which he blamed himself for. He carried her through to his bedroom and lay her on his bed. "Please lie with me, I'm frightened," she sobbed. "Amira, that would be wrong, we hardly know each other. We are strangers." "Don't you like me?" she asked. "Yes, I like you very much, but because you have been drinking, this might not be what you really want. I don't want you to regret something that happened while you were not in full control." "But I want it to happen, I've dreamt about this every day since I first met you."

Beyani didn't know how to handle this situation. He was a doctor who had allowed a patient in his company to over-indulge in alcohol. Now she wanted him to lie with her. Could he restrain himself if he lay next to her? Would she want more from him? Would he want more from her? It was a precarious situation. "Please, Beyani, come lie with me and hold me in your arms," she called to him. What did his heart tell him? 'Yes, go to her,' this is right for you both. He fetched a cover and laid it over her, then took his shoes off and lay down beside her. He felt her arms reaching for him so he moved closer. She started to sob so he took her in his arms. They were both still fully clothed. It didn't take long for them both to drop off to sleep in each other's arms.

During the night Amira stirred thinking she was in a dream, so slipped her clothes off, wondering why she was in bed fully clothed. Her naked body lay next to Beyani's. When he woke through the night, he was shocked to find Amira's naked body next to his. She was still asleep, so he undressed and climbed back into bed. His hands accidentally touched her breasts. They were soft and he gently caressed them. His hands moved over her body, then down her thighs. His heart was racing and his body aching, he wanted this brave young woman. He knew this from the first moment he set eyes on her; they had things in common, things that needed to be shared. Was this the right time?

Amira stirred as she felt hands moving down by her private area, then she let out a scream. She was having a flashback to her begging days. Beyani was startled. Did she not want this to happen? "Amira, it's me, do you not want me to touch you?" She sat up in bed and burst out crying. "I'm sorry, I thought it was that horrible soldier touching me. Yes, Beyani, please love me," she pleaded, as she lay down and snuggled into him. His hands gently caressed her body. She had not felt such gentleness before; this was real, it was happening right now, and her body was tingling. She wasn't sure what happened next, but whatever it was, made her let out a squeal of delight. Then the sandman visited them again and off to sleep they went.

Beyani was the first to stir in the morning. Had he dreamt about last night? No, because there was Amira lying naked beside him. He leaned over to kiss her, thus waking her up. She struggled up in the bed and couldn't believe what she saw: here was her doctor lying naked beside her. Why was she here in his bed? Her mind went totally blank. What had happened last night? "Why am I here?" she asked. Beyani didn't know what to say. Did she not remember what they had done together? Had he taken her against her better judgment? He felt sick, a doctor just didn't do these things to a patient. Amira rubbed her eyes, then she started to recall what had happened. It was her who had asked to be made love to. She suddenly felt embarrassed. "Thank you for a wonderful night, you were so gentle with me." "Surely that wasn't your first time, Amira, why didn't you tell me?" he asked. "I didn't want you to refuse me." No one had taken from the other what they didn't want to give, it was by mutual consent, and this put Beyani's mind at rest.

They both climbed out of bed, but a little pain in her shoulder made Amira flinch. Had she hurt it while making love last night? Beyani noticed the look on her face so told her to stay in bed. He would get himself some breakfast then go to the hospital. There in the dining room was last night's dinner untouched, so he covered it and put it in the safe. He smiled to himself. Was this the girl he had been waiting on, had she arrived at last? They would have last night's dinner tonight, but he would certainly hide the alcohol! He went to the bedroom before he left and kissed her forehead. She slept on.

When Amira woke, she lay in bed and hugged the pillow, the one her doctor had laid his head on. What a night, it all came flooding back to her, but what about the dinner date? It had gone horribly wrong — no food was eaten, instead she had over-indulged in the alcohol department. How disrespectful of her! She made herself some toast, then walked to the hospital to see Roserin.

Meanwhile Beyani had called in to attend to Roserin's bandages. Her legs had been hit with shrapnel, but thank goodness they were not deep wounds. He was worried about infection, as the hospital was operating on emergency services. "Did you have a nice night with Amira?" she asked. "Yes, we enjoyed ourselves." "Did you kiss her?" The poor doctor blushed. He was taken by surprise with these in-your-face questions and was not prepared. "Well, yes," he stammered.

"Then she must be your girlfriend now?" asked Roserin. "That will be enough questions for now, young lady, just you concentrate on getting better," he told her. "As soon as I am healed, I'm going to join Amira and her comrades. We will take out those ISIS snipers. I hate them, they took my parents from me, now I only have her left," and with this she started to cry. The doctor sat and held her hand. "One day you will be a brave warrior like Amira, the two of you will be fine together." This brought a smile to her sad face.

On saying this Beyani had second thoughts. Was he

falling in love with Amira? If so, he would be worried about her being a militant. It was a dangerous job, not one he would be happy with her being part of. But that was a long way off, and so many things could happen before then. He would just have to be patient. His thoughts were broken when he saw Amira walking down the corridor towards Roserin's bed. He watched as she kissed her, then she sat down beside her and held her hand. "How are you today, my pet?" "The doctor said he kissed you last night so he must be your boyfriend?" was what greeted her. Amira blushed; how did she know what had happened? "You are only guessing?" Roserin was adamant. "No, the doctor told me so." The subject was quickly dropped when Amira asked her what she had planned for the future. "I'm going to be a soldier; I'm coming with you when I get better. The doctor said you and I are very brave."

Tonight, Amira would again spend it with Beyani. This time they would keep their dinner date, so ate the reheated meal from last night. He didn't offer any drinks, as he wanted her to be in total control of her thoughts and feelings. This would be their last night together as they were going their separate ways tomorrow. They lay together and caressed each other. This was the first time Amira had touched a man and she was worried, but it just seemed a natural process so her worries were unfounded. Neither wanted the night to end; it was long and passionate and took their minds away from their work commitments. Tomorrow would bring with it sad goodbyes.

8

DUTY CALLS AMIRA BACK

AMIRA SAID her goodbyes to both Beyani and Roserin, as she was needed back at headquarters, but unbeknown to Beyani she was crossing back into Syria. A new spate of fighting had broken out, as ISIS soldiers were advancing on all towns in their path. They needed all the fighters they could get, and Amira being one of their deadliest snipers was needed on the front line. Her shoulder was a worry, but if she had a comrade that would reload her rifle when needed, she would do her very best. Some of the American troops had arrived, and for this they were grateful, but the largest contingent had arrived in Iraq, where they were going to establish a 'safe haven' that included most areas of Kurdish settlements in northern Iraq. This was, for the most part, freedom from interference by the Iraqi government.

In Syria, Kurdish fighters were essential allies to America, pushing far beyond their own area to eradicate the caliphate (Muslim rule) that had been so key to ISIS recruitment. This was why Amira's militants were needed — they would join up with their Syrian counterparts and form one big army. She now had two reasons to live, so would not take unnecessary risks. They were in touch with the PYD (the Democratic Union Party), who used weapons manufactured in Western countries. For their part, the Kurds were promised their own national country by the European states and the USA, for being their allies against ISIS.

Amira was given a commander's position within her military party, as she was invaluable in the tracking of ISIS snipers. She would take her comrades to the outskirts and settle them in bombed-out ruins, then lie in wait. She knew ISIS planned to attack when darkness descended, so they were ready. Their military equipment was far more up-to-date than the Kurds', but if they could take them down as they were setting up, then it didn't matter who had what! To take them out was all that mattered.

Near midnight there was movement and snipers could be seen advancing in their direction, but until Amira gave the 'Fire one' and then the 'Fire two' commands, they had to remain in their positions. She knew to pick off as many as possible she had to let them get quite close, although it was frightening. Suddenly, out rang the first command, 'Fire one!' and the first line of her militants let fire, picking them off one by one, as they were not expecting an attacked. Then 'Fire two!' rang out and another round of shots was fired, so more ISIS snipers were wiped out. A successful mission was accomplished. But all was not over as an eerie silence reigned — ISIS always had back-up. Amira quickly moved her soldiers nearer the city; a new position would leave ISIS wondering as to their whereabouts. They would hunker down for however long it took. This was their life, living conditions were less than adequate, but they had been trained that their people and country came first; they were militants first and foremost! One dead ISIS sniper was one less to bring harm to their people.

Meanwhile, on the other side of the city, American troops were in an all-out war against ISIS. Shells and mortars were penetrating the inner city, where pockets of civilians were huddled together as they were unable to get out or hide from all that was happening around them. They were mainly women and children, the innocent ones caught up in this barbaric crossfire. There was no mercy, it was all about ISIS eradicating the Kurds as they had become America's allies. Amid all this, people were starving and the world was alerted to the people's suffering. This brought about a twelve-day truce, so armies could get food to the people trapped in the midst of all the fighting. Many civilians decided to leave and flee to the Bardarash camp, a desolate refugee camp that already contained Kurds from Syria who had earlier fled the country.

Amira and her comrades were the undercover snipers. They didn't become involved in the main action. Their job was to pick off the ISIS snipers that had embedded themselves in the outer ruins, committing horrific crimes —

shooting families as they tried to escape. She had seen this many times. These innocent people were shot in cold-blooded, calculated attacks. These horrific killings by ISIS was the main reason why the YPJ were formed in the first place, as most of these women were traumatised themselves, having lost family members to this brutal regime. It was months before Amira was able to get back to see Beyani and Roserin again. She missed them dearly, and not being able to communicate made it more difficult, as they didn't know if she was dead or alive.

Meanwhile Beyani was worried sick for Amira, but his job at the hospital kept his mind busy, as new casualties arrived every day. He had to perform surgery on some horrific injuries. Some surgeries were successful, others not, but he had learnt to live with this — it was life in a war zone. Roserin was now helping out at the hospital; her injuries were healing nicely. Doctor Beyani had arranged for her to have a room in his apartment block, as she was an orphan and was special to him and Amira. When Amira walked in, they were both excited that she had come back alive. Roserin wanted to know where she had been and how many ISIS snipers she had shot. This was still her aim, to work alongside her hero! Beyani, on the other hand, didn't want to know about her fighting; he had more important things on his mind. That she had come back was enough for him. Tonight, they would lay side by side and hold each other in their arms, then make love until the small hours of the morning! He had missed her so much and now knew: he couldn't live without her. This was the one he had been waiting for, and he wasn't about to let her go.

It only took two weeks before Amira was called up to join her comrades, as they had another assignment, which would take them back into Syria. This time she had a new comrade, as Roserin had been in tears begging to go with her. Amira asked Beyani what he thought about her joining the YPJ, as she was still a child, only eleven years old. "If it is her calling, we can't stop her. She, like you, has suffered at the hands of ISIS. You wanted revenge, so does she!" Amira thanked him for being so understanding. "I will miss you. It gets harder each time we part, but one day we will be together as a couple," she promised. Roserin was excited about becoming a militant; hopefully it would come up to her expectations, but this did worry Amira a little.

The keenness soon subsided from Roserin's enthusiasm when she saw the conditions they were expected to camp in. There was no such thing as furniture, instead slabs of concrete or flat pieces of timber, anything really that was salvageable, became their seating arrangements. She would learn quickly that her reason for becoming a militant was to fight for the Kurdish people, and living rough was part of the glory. "I'm happy you are here with me, Amira, otherwise I wouldn't like it here on my own," she admitted. Tears were visible in her eyes. This was obviously not what she had imagined, but Amira had warned her it was not a glamorous job, in fact far from it.

They hunkered down in the ruins, as they weren't

expecting anything to happen tonight, but this meant nothing — they always had to be alert. Tonight, two guards were in place, as uncertainty could be cause for concern. This was new territory and ISIS snipers had been spotted in the vicinity. It wasn't long before there was movement in their refuge. They were all accounted for, so who was there besides them? Had ISIS snipers infiltrated their ruins without warning? Was this an ambush? Amira quickly pulled Roserin close to her and gave her a knife in case she was attacked. "Have no pity — one enemy sniper dead is one less to harm our people. Use it if you have to," she whispered.

Suddenly it all happened: ISIS snipers were in the ruins with them. When they opened fire, Amira gave the command 'Fire one!' and an array of crossfire was exchanged, then 'Fire two!' took the ISIS snipers by surprise as they had exposed themselves, so they became easy targets. This was when the knives came out, to make sure they didn't survive. Wounded snipers could still be dangerous. Amira told Roserin to follow her to where several wounded men lay. She told her to knife them in the chest while she picked up their rifles. Poor Roserin froze, so Amira grabbed the knife and finished them off. Roserin was in shock, her hero had turned into a killer. She started to cry, but she had to learn quickly. It was either her or them. There were no choices … it was simple, life or death?

This was the first time her comrades had been so close to death, although several had been unaccounted for, so it was a matter of waiting to see if they returned. Several hours had passed and they were two comrades down, so Amira decided to scout the ruins to see if she could find them. The sisterhood rule was if anyone was badly wounded, they were not to be left alive to be tortured by ISIS snipers, so this had to be obeyed. Roserin followed Amira as she was worried for her. She had a knife if danger lurked … but could she use it? It didn't take long for her to spot a sniper. She was right behind him and he had his gun pointed at Amira. It was too late to warn her so this left one option: she had to take him out, otherwise Amira would be shot. She lunged forward and stabbed him in the back. He slumped over and his rifle fell to the ground. She picked up the rifle and fired at him just to make sure he was dead. "Good girl, Roserin, you saved my life. See, if it is a matter of life or death, we don't have choices, we have to act." There would be no going back for her now. She had saved her hero's life, so saw how vulnerable life was … it was all or nothing.

They kept searching for their lost comrades until they came across them. One had died and the other was badly wounded. This was going to be the hardest lesson for Roserin. Amira assessed the situation and knew it was just a matter of time, but she couldn't risk leaving her alive at the mercy of ISIS snipers. She bent down and whispered something to her, then picked up her rifle and fired the fatal shot. Roserin stood frozen to the spot. She had witnessed Amira shoot one of her own. The tears flowed and for one moment, her hero had turned into a killer. How could she do that, kill one of her own? "I hate you!" she sobbed, and turned to run away. Amira caught her and gently slapped her face. "Roserin, we cannot leave our comrades at the mercy of the enemy. They would use torture, her death would be brutal. This is the sisterhood rule, everyone has to abide by it. One day you will have to do the same. I know it is unethical, but the alternative is far worse. I have seen what they do to women. Islamic soldiers class women as subservient, we are just commodities to them, and to be killed by a woman in their eyes would mean the worst humiliation and shame. Don't be angry with me, this is what life is like on the front line. Sometimes we do things that aren't normal, but life isn't normal when fighting ISIS. They are murderers. Think back to your own parents — no mercy was shown to them." Slowly Roserin began to understand why she was here and what was expected of her as a soldier. Could she become that hardcore person like her hero? She would try.

Many more months were spent in crossfire with ISIS, and with each confrontation, Roserin adjusted to the situations they found themselves in. But she had noticed that Amira was not well and this worried her. She would wander off in the mornings to be by herself, so she followed her one morning, only to find her vomiting. "Amira, what is wrong? Are you ill?" she asked. "I am pregnant with Beyani's baby." What a shock to Roserin and also to Amira when she realised what was wrong. She had never thought of the consequences of their lovemaking, but now she had to confront the reality. "What are you going to do?" asked Roserin. "I thought being a sniper was my life, but now I have another person to consider, so I will have to leave soon, as it won't be safe for me in this condition. But I have one last thing to do and that is to train you to be a leader. You are showing promise, now that you fully understand our cause and our sisterhood rules. You are still young, so you can only grow with age and with the experience your comrades will teach you. They will care for and look after you." Roserin turned away to hide her tears. She loved Amira. How was she going to live without her? No words could describe how much she would miss her, so she put her arms around her and held on for dear life. This spoke volumes.

The time had come for Amira to leave her comrades and return to Beyani. Roserin cried. She looked upon Amira as a mother figure, although there was only twelve years' difference in their ages, but she knew it was too dangerous for her to remain there without proper medical care. What would Doctor Beyani think when he saw Amira's extended belly? She knew he loved Amira, but not to know he was about to be a father, how would he feel?

It took three days for Amira to make it back to the hospital where Beyani worked. She hoped he would be happy with the news she was going to break to him. As she walked towards him, he was so happy she had come back alive. Then he noticed something different about her. "Amira, thank God you are safe, I've missed you. Is this our baby? Why didn't you come home sooner?" he asked in disbelief. She took him in her arms to let him feel the change in her body. Was he ready for this? "I never thought of the consequences of our love affair until I realised I was pregnant. I was shocked to begin with, but as time went by, I began to accept that from love a new life is about to be born. I hope you are as happy as me, Beyani?" she asked. He held her, telling her it was the best news, he was so happy. They both shared tears of joy. "You go home and I will there as soon as I finish here, then we will have to make plans for the future."

That night they lay in each other's arms where they both felt they belonged. He had to ask the burning question; it was eating him inside. "Does this mean your days as a sniper are over and you will not be returning to the YPJ camp?" "I cannot just walk out, as Roserin is now entrenched in the movement. I will continue to supply information, but my fighting days are over. I worry about our people, the way they are treated. Will we ever get our Kurdish state as promised? Our work in war-torn Syria and neighbouring countries including Iraq was to help make a better future for the Kurdish people, but we are still a long way off from a peaceful solution. The US put their troops in to rid ISIS terrorists, but without the Kurds they could not have done this. They needed us, and with this came promises, but so far none has been kept. What will happen to us, Beyani? I'm frightened," she sobbed. "Worrying is not going to solve anything. We have a baby to think about. Don't be sidetracked by warfare. We just have to live with hope that one day things will change for the better."

9

A NEW LIFE AND RENEWED HOPE

A NEW LIFE HAD EMERGED: a little boy was born to Amira and Beyani. They were proud parents. Their life was better than most because of Beyani's position at the hospital. At least they had somewhere to live, not like thousands of other Kurdish people. Amira asked if she could call their baby Behaz, after her younger brother who was taken prisoner by ISIS. Amira had no information on either of her siblings. Had they survived the horrors of war? she wondered. One could only live in hope!

She still played a role in the YPJ movement, supplying information as to the whereabouts of the American troops and how they had taken out many ISIS cells. The facts were that ISIS had lost most of the territory it controlled in Syria because of the local Syrian Kurds who fought them. There were six American casualties in the five years of fighting, while Syrian Kurds lost close to 11,000 fighters and many more were wounded.

As baby Behaz grew and two more siblings arrived, nothing much had changed in the fight for a Kurdish state. Amira was still heavily involved with the YPJ movement and passed what information she could on to Roserin, who was now a commander in the women's army.

Then one day the shock news that dampened the hopes of the Kurdish people. The American president, Mr Trump, on 6 October had a conversation with Turkey's president, then abruptly ordered United States forces to abandon their positions protecting Syrian Kurds, who had been their essential allies in the common fight against ISIS. This now opened up a gateway, enabling a Turkish invasion, thus double-crossing the Syrian Kurds who were their allies for five years against the Islamic State group. Now the Kurds again found themselves as fighters, to try to secure a future for their people.

The American pull-out marked the start of a complex and hard-to-understand new phase in which foreign powers Russia and Turkey rushed into the void left by the Americans. This made Amira and her YPJ movement angry, as during the Iraq invasion, the USA was very careful to keep the Kurds on their side. Would history have been different if they had the Kurds as enemies?

The promise made by European states and the USA to the Kurds about having their own nation country had not been kept, so they felt betrayed! The Kurdish militia would fight on for the cause, for their people to have a state of their own. Since the USA pull-out, Turkish troops have been shelling Kurdish homes in Syria. As Turkish forces push forward, they execute people leaving them lying in ditches along the roadside, thus causing 160,000 civilians to flee, most going deeper into Syria, others making their way east to Iraq. Many believe Turkey's ultimate aim is to drive Kurds out. Kurdish lands were duly seized without authority and transferred to thousands of Arabs resettled by the state, in their place!

Prior to the Turkish occupation, life under the Kurdish-run administration was good, as there was peace, order and stability. Now the Arab proxies (people who are authorised to act on behalf of someone else) in the National Syrian Army face no such censure as they themselves are corrupt, occupying and looting Kurdish homes. The YPJ movement are shocked and angry as their people are labelled 'pigs' and 'infidels' (infidels meaning people who are of a different religion or who have no religion). The Turkish 'proxy' shares a long hatred against the Kurds and is the most oppressive state in the region.

The YPJ movement know how instrumental their success in contributing along with other Kurdish fighters was in the fight against ISIS, but now for the American troops to abandon them and leave them to die is a big mistake by the US. Trump's betrayal leads the Kurdish people to believe that the great power has been double-dipping since 1923, when the treaty that gave them a country (dubbed 'Kurdistan') was overtaken by a treaty that erased it. If Turkey — which directly aided ISIS on many occasions in the past and which relies on its Syrian jihadist proxies — conquers the Kurdish areas of Syria, all the gains that were once made will be lost and it will be back to where it all started. New cells of Jihadists will start again and infiltrate these countries and bring back the horror that once reigned.

Mr Trump simply gave in to the Turkish threats … but why? This was his reckoning: 'We have spent tremendous amounts of money on helping the Kurds in terms of ammunition, in terms of weapons, in terms of money …', along with more of his petty reasoning! He had the audacity to add, 'With all that said, we like the Kurds.' How barbaric, how pitiful, when so many Kurds died helping American troops to wipe out ISIS. Now they are meant to be grateful for America's help, for what? Through all the bloodshed, what has been gained?

What America did was satisfy Turkish demands for a safe zone, getting the Kurds to dismantle their fortifications near the Turkish border, which leaves it open for Turkey to invade northeastern Syria. There was no resolve for the Kurds in this matter and nothing was done to prevent a Turkish invasion. It is a disaster that is already happening!

Amira and her comrades' fight will never end. The Kurdish militant groups will fight until they have, at the very least, a Kurdish zone, if not a Kurdish state, so they can maintain their own language and culture. "Is this too much to want for our people?" asked Amira.

Does America not feel it has betrayed the Kurds? Where is the justice in all this? Perhaps a day of reckoning is on the horizon.

ABOUT THE AUTHOR

Margaret Nyhon lives in Alexandra, in the Central Otago province of New Zealand, where she writes, paints and practises the crafts of printing and bookbinding. She has worked extensively in hospitality management in New Zealand and resort management in Australia. The urge to trace her family history led her to the writing of her first non-fiction work, de Marisco. She has since written several fiction and non-fiction works. Margaret is married and has three adult children and two grandsons.

Non-fiction

de Marisco

Freedom Knows No Boundaries

A Wake-up Call

A Shattered Dream Across the Tasman

Fiction

Isobella (Book 1 in the *Isobella* series)

Isobella: Self Redemption (Book 2 in the *Isobella* series)

Papa's Girl Emmeline

Betrayal by an Irish Rose

Revenge for an English Lord (sequel to Betrayal by an Irish Rose)

For Girls' Eyes Only

Daughters Lost to the Underworld